"I want to be with... you."

"And I want you to be with me, my precious," replied the Earl. "But God knows what we are going to do about each other."

Lydia had forgotten her sister and that the Earl was engaged to her, forgotten everything except that they were alone in Paradise, that he had his arms around her and had kissed her...

"You must know, my darling one," the Earl continued quietly, "that I love you."

Lydia looked up at him in speechless astonishment.

"But we are both aware that the real question is— what can we do about it?"

THE ISLAND OF LOVE

A Camfield Novel of Love

Dearest Reader,

Camfield Novels of Love mark a very exciting era of my books with Jove. They already have nearly two hundred of my books which they have had ever since they became my first publisher in America. Now all my original paperback romances in the future will be published by them.

As you already know, Camfield Place in Hertfordshire is my home, which originally existed in 1275, but was rebuilt in 1867 by the grandfather of Beatrix Potter.

It was here in this lovely house, with the best view of the county, that she wrote *The Tale of Peter Rabbit*. Mr. McGregor's garden is exactly as she described it. The door in the wall that the fat little rabbit could not squeeze underneath and the goldfish pool where the white cat sat twitching its tail are still there.

I had Camfield Place blessed when I came here in 1950 and was so happy with my husband until he died, and now with my children and grandchildren, that I know the atmosphere is filled with love and we have all been very lucky.

It is easy here to write of love and I know you will enjoy the Camfield Novels of Love. Their plots are definitely exciting and the covers very romantic. They come to you, like all my books, with love.

Bless you,

Books by Barbara Cartland

THE ADVENTURER
AGAIN THIS RAPTURE
ARMOUR AGAINST
    LOVE
THE AUDACIOUS
    ADVENTURESS
BARBARA CARTLAND'S
    BOOK OF BEAUTY
    AND HEALTH
THE BITTER WINDS OF
    LOVE
BLUE HEATHER
BROKEN BARRIERS
THE CAPTIVE HEART
THE COIN OF LOVE
THE COMPLACENT WIFE
COUNT THE STARS
CUPID RIDES PILLION
DANCE ON MY HEART
DESIRE OF THE HEART
DESPERATE DEFIANCE
THE DREAM WITHIN
A DUEL OF HEARTS
ELIZABETH EMPRESS OF
    AUSTRIA
ELIZABETHAN LOVER
THE ENCHANTED
    MOMENT
THE ENCHANTED
    WALTZ
THE ENCHANTING EVIL
ESCAPE FROM PASSION
FOR ALL ETERNITY
A GHOST IN MONTE
    CARLO
THE GOLDEN GONDOLA
A HALO FOR THE DEVIL
A HAZARD OF HEARTS
A HEART IS BROKEN
THE HEART OF THE
    CLAN
THE HIDDEN EVIL
THE HIDDEN HEART
THE HORIZONS OF LOVE
AN INNOCENT IN
    MAYFAIR
IN THE ARMS OF LOVE

THE IRRESISTIBLE BUCK
JOSEPHINE EMPRESS OF
    FRANCE
THE KISS OF PARIS
THE KISS OF THE DEVIL
A KISS OF SILK
THE KNAVE OF HEARTS
THE LEAPING FLAME
A LIGHT TO THE HEART
LIGHTS OF LOVE
THE LITTLE PRETENDER
LOST ENCHANTMENT
LOST LOVE
LOVE AND LINDA
LOVE AT FORTY
LOVE FORBIDDEN
LOVE HOLDS THE
    CARDS
LOVE IN HIDING
LOVE IN PITY
LOVE IS AN EAGLE
LOVE IS CONTRABAND
LOVE IS DANGEROUS
LOVE IS MINE
LOVE IS THE ENEMY
LOVE ME FOREVER
LOVE ON THE RUN
LOVE TO THE RESCUE
LOVE UNDER FIRE
THE MAGIC OF HONEY
MESSENGER OF LOVE
METTERNICH: THE
    PASSIONATE
    DIPLOMAT
MONEY, MAGIC AND
    MARRIAGE
NO HEART IS FREE
THE ODIOUS DUKE
OPEN WINGS
OUT OF REACH
THE PASSIONATE
    PILGRIM
THE PRETTY
    HORSEBREAKERS
THE PRICE IS LOVE
A RAINBOW TO HEAVEN
THE RELUCTANT BRIDE

THE RUNAWAY HEART
THE SCANDALOUS LIFE
    OF KING CAROL
THE SECRET FEAR
THE SMUGGLED HEART
A SONG OF LOVE
STARS IN MY HEART
STOLEN HALO
SWEET ADVENTURE
SWEET ENCHANTRESS
SWEET PUNISHMENT
THEFT OF A HEART
THE THIEF OF LOVE
THIS TIME IT'S LOVE
TOUCH A STAR
TOWARDS THE STARS
THE UNKNOWN HEART
THE UNPREDICTABLE
    BRIDE
A VIRGIN IN PARIS
WE DANCED ALL NIGHT
WHERE IS LOVE?
THE WINGS OF ECSTASY
THE WINGS OF LOVE
WINGS ON MY HEART
WOMAN, THE ENIGMA

CAMFIELD NOVELS OF LOVE

THE POOR GOVERNESS
WINGED VICTORY
LUCKY IN LOVE
LOVE AND THE MARQUIS
A MIRACLE IN MUSIC
LIGHT OF THE GODS
BRIDE TO A BRIGAND
LOVE COMES WEST
A WITCH'S SPELL
SECRETS
THE STORMS OF LOVE
MOONLIGHT ON THE
    SPHINX
WHITE LILAC
REVENGE OF THE HEART
THE ISLAND OF LOVE

A NEW CAMFIELD NOVEL OF LOVE BY

BARBARA CARTLAND

The Island of Love

A JOVE BOOK

THE ISLAND OF LOVE

A Jove Book/published by arrangement with
the author

PRINTING HISTORY
Jove edition/November 1984

ISBN: 0-515-07911-1

Jove books are published by The Berkley Publishing Group,
200 Madison Avenue, New York, N.Y. 10016.
The words "A JOVE BOOK" and the "J" with sunburst
are trademarks belonging to Jove Publications, Inc.

PRINTED IN THE UNITED STATES OF AMERICA

Author's Note

When I visited Hawaii in 1983, I found it very, very beautiful. I saw the Iolani Palace built by the 'Merry Monarch,' King Kalakaua and the famous Waikiki beach. In 1889 His Majesty lent the Royal Beach House, which I mention in this novel, to Robert Louis Stevenson.

The author was, on his arrival in Hawaii, greeted as a celebrity and struck up a warm friendship with the King and they frequently gave *luaus* and informal parties for each other.

The details of King Kalakaua's Coronation which lasted for two weeks, are correct and it took place in 1883, nine years after he had been elected to the throne by the Legislative Assembly.

Hawaii although over-built and over-populated is still magical, and when at Diamond Point I looked out at dawn and dusk I found myself saying:

Stars like diamonds in the sable sky
Light the murmurous soft Hawaiian sea.

The Island of Love

chapter one

1883

Sir Robert Westbury came into the Morning-Room where his two daughters were arguing.

This was nothing unusual because, whatever Lydia said, her sister Heloise always contradicted it.

After years of trying to placate Heloise, Lydia had found it was simplest to agree to what she said and thereby prevent, what she often thought, was an undignified and rather vulgar exchange of words.

Heloise Westbury was so beautiful that from the moment she became aware of her own face she felt the world was made for her to walk on.

She was about fifteen when she realised she had only to look at a man from under her long eye-lashes for him to talk to her in a different tone from the one he had been using before, and to have what she often described to Lydia as a "swimming look in his eyes."

Last year when she had appeared in London as a débutante, she had been acclaimed, fêted and extolled by everybody except the girls of her own age who were trying to compete with her.

She had come back reluctantly to the country for Christmas only slightly appeased by the certainty that she would be the Belle of every Hunt Ball, and that a great number of her admirers in London contrived to stay either at Westbury Park if Heloise could arrange an invitation for them, or at other houses in the neighbourhood.

All this meant a great deal more work for Lydia who, since her father had become a widower for the second time, had run the house for him besides being expected to dance attendance on her half-sister.

Lydia's mother had died soon after she was born and Sir Robert had quickly married again, hoping for an heir to the Baronetcy.

He would have been even more disappointed if Heloise had not been so lovely even when she was in the cradle, that it had been a compensation to know, when he learnt that his wife unfortunately could give him no more children, that at least he had an exceptional and outstandingly lovely daughter.

Although it was very unfair, he vented his anger and disappointment on his elder daughter rather than on his second child.

"Why could you not have been a son?" he would ask furiously. "It would have simplified everything!"

"I am sorry, Papa," was all Lydia could say meekly.

She thought at times that he looked at her with positive dislike because she would not be able to follow in his footsteps and become the fifth Baronet.

Although she tried to tell herself sensibly that this was something she could not help, it often preyed on her mind.

When two years ago her Stepmother had died after a long, lingering illness during which time she would ordinarily have made her own début, she hoped that her father would marry for the third time.

He had, however, last year when mourning was over, seemed to be obsessed with presenting Heloise to the Social World.

Lydia thought that perhaps once Heloise was safely married she would have another Stepmother, and then there might be a chance of escape from what had become a monotonous treadmill.

All day long it was: "Tell Lydia to do that!"—"Why does not Lydia see to the arrangements as she should do?"—"Send for Lydia!"

If the food was not appetising enough, if the gardeners had neglected part of the garden, if the footmen failed in their duties, it was Lydia who had to cope with it.

It was Lydia who had to soothe down ruffled feelings and especially to keep her father from losing his temper.

It was not surprising that she was very thin and there was a permanently worried expression in her large eyes.

She never had time to think about herself, and if she did she merely shrugged her shoulders and said truthfully that nobody would look at her when Heloise was there.

Heloise was every man's ideal of what a young English girl should look like.

"She is a perfect 'English Rose,'" was how her admirers described her and it was an accurate description.

She had hair the colour of ripening corn, eyes as blue as a summer sky, and her complexion was the perfect pink and white that every artist aspired to put on canvas.

It was unfortunate that when the fairies bestowed their gifts on her at her christening two qualities had been inexplicably missing.

Nobody who lived with Heloise for long could have failed to realise that she was not very intelligent.

She never read a book and her conversation was limited to one subject—herself.

What was more, 'unselfishness' was a word that could not be found in her vocabulary, and certainly not in her heart.

"I am tired, Heloise," Lydia had said to her once, having run up and down the stairs for what seemed like a hundred times before Heloise was finally ready to attend a Ball.

"Tired?" her half-sister had repeated. "Why should you be tired? Anyway, it is your duty to look after me and do as I want."

Lydia wanted to ask why, but she knew it would only annoy Heloise who would then be very rude and fly into one of her tantrums which upset everybody except herself.

Now as Sir Robert came into the Morning-Room the girls' voices faded away.

Lydia's cheeks were a little flushed with the argument, Heloise was looking sulky and her Cupid's-bow lips were turned down at the corners.

Sir Robert walked across to where they were sitting in the window and said:

"A note has just been brought to me by a groom. You have pulled it off, Heloise!"

"I have, Papa?"

Heloise gave a scream of excitement and jumped up from the table.

"Tell me what he says!"

"The Earl has asked for my permission to pay his addresses to you," Sir Robert replied, "and hopes he may call this afternoon to discuss with me a very important matter."

Heloise gave another scream.

"Oh, Papa, I was so afraid, even after what he said at the Ball last night, that he would not come up to scratch!"

"Well, he has, and I am delighted, my dearest," Sir Robert said, "and very, very proud of you!"

He put his arm round his daughter and kissed her cheek.

Lydia who was watching realised that Heloise stiffened in case he should crease her gown or untidy her hair.

Then she asked quietly:

"Are you saying, Papa, that the Earl of Royston has proposed to Heloise?"

"He has asked my permission to do so," Sir Robert replied.

"It is wonderful! I am so happy!" Heloise cried. "I shall be a Countess, with a traditional position at Court, besides being hostess at Royston Abbey and all the other houses the Earl owns."

She spoke with a lilt in her voice which made it

sound almost an exaltation.

"I am so glad, Heloise, that you will be happy," Lydia said.

"Happy? Of course I shall be happy!" Heloise retorted. "This is what I have been working for, for a long time. Of course I was quite certain I would get him in the end."

She did not notice Lydia wince as if the way she spoke jarred on her.

Sir Robert glanced down at the note in his hand.

"I am going to answer this," he said, "and tell Royston we shall look forward to seeing him at teatime. We must certainly have a bottle of champagne ready on ice to celebrate!"

"Yes, of course, Papa," Heloise agreed. "But mind that you leave him alone with me first. He has not asked me formally and that is what I want to hear."

"It is formal enough for me to announce your engagement in the *Gazette*," Sir Robert replied in a tone of satisfaction.

He walked out of the room as he spoke and when the door had closed behind him Heloise said:

"There! I told you I would marry the most important man in England, and that is what I am going to do!"

"Do you love him, Heloise?"

There was just a little pause before Heloise replied:

"Where marriage is concerned, it is important to marry a man in the right position."

Lydia looked at her half-sister searchingly before she said:

"You did not think of that yourself. It is something Lady Burton taught you."

but the most docile of horses and to go further than the Park.

"If I had a son he would appreciate the way I have built up my racing-stables, and acquired some of the finest hunters in the County!" Sir Robert often said. "They are wasted on women! Absolutely wasted!"

This was not true as far as Lydia was concerned, but then she did not count, and she knew that her father genuinely did not realise what a good rider she was.

She could control, as well as he could, any horse, however wild.

When she had first seen the Earl of Royston she had realised that he was exactly how she thought a man should look.

It was not only that he was extremely handsome and undoubtedly a brilliant rider, but also that he had a fascinating buccaneering face that complemented his reputation.

He looked, Lydia told herself, rather like the explorers and English pirates must have done in the Reign of Queen Elizabeth when they had gone out to discover new worlds, fight the Spaniards, and bring home cargoes of treasure richer than anything that had ever been seen before.

Watching the Earl in the hunting-field, she had thought that he should in fact, be galloping towards new and distant horizons, rather than being confined as it seemed, by the small English fields, the social life of the County, or even that of London.

Only once had she dined in the same room with him, and that was when he had come to dinner at Sir

Robert's house in London, before a Ball that was being given for Heloise.

As the most important person present, he had sat on her right, and looking at them sitting side-by-side Lydia thought it would be impossible anywhere in the world to find two people who were each so outstandingly beautiful in their own way.

This she knew was a strange adjective to apply to a man.

Yet it seemed fitting because the Earl had so positive a personality and his whole being was far more arresting than that of any other man she had ever seen.

She had however learned more about him, and what she heard was not altogether surprising.

At twenty-nine he had turned the heads of a great number of beautiful women and captured their hearts.

He was celebrated for being convincibly elusive and every ambitious Mother had known even before they started the chase that they had no hope of catching him.

Because he was a great landowner and possessed some of the finest race-horses in England, as well as being an outstanding sportsman who held a great number of personal trophies to show for it, other men admired and envied him.

But it had never entered Lydia's mind for a moment that he might marry Heloise.

Lydia did not herself talk very much, as nobody seemed to wish to hear what she had to say, but she was a sympathetic listener.

The Earl because he lived near them, was a frequent topic of conversation in the country, and in London his various love-affairs were agreeable tid-bits of gossip.

Lydia learnt more and more about him, until she felt that she could write a book about the Earl of Royston, and still fill another two volumes.

Everything about him was intriguing, and perhaps even his nickname by which he was always known had added to the aura that encircled him.

The story was that when he was born his father was out hunting, and a groom was sent from the Abbey to inform His Lordship that he had an heir.

Unfortunately, breathless from the speed at which he had ridden and also rather nervous of his master, the groom blurted out the news to which the Earl listened without a great deal of interest.

Then as he turned away the man asked:

"Is there any message for Her Ladyship, M'Lord?"

For a moment the Earl looked at him in surprise. Then he said:

"Good God! Are you telling me that it is Her Ladyship who has given birth? I thought it was one of my hunters!"

This statement was overheard by several of his friends who roared with laughter.

Then one of them said:

"If he is your son, undoubtedly he will be a good hunter, and what could be a better name for him?"

The present Earl of Royston had therefore always been known as 'Hunter,' and the more Lydia heard about him the more she thought the nickname appropriate.

He hunted, not only foxes, but also beautiful

women, although she had the feeling that once the chase was over he was often no longer interested.

And yet now, although it seemed incredible, without very much of a run for his money he had hunted and caught Heloise.

"You are very lucky!" Lydia said aloud.

As she spoke she wondered if in fact, Heloise was as lucky as everybody would think she was.

Heloise was however so excited that she forgot for a moment her affectations.

"I am to be married, Lydia!"

She danced around the room, her full skirt swinging out, making her look so graceful and so lovely that she might have stepped down from Olympus to bemuse poor mortals.

Then she sat down in a chair and said:

"I must start planning my trousseau. I shall have the most glorious clothes that any bride has ever possessed, and when my friends see them, they will be green with envy!"

"When do you think you will be married?" Lydia asked.

"As soon as possible!" Heloise replied.

Then she hesitated.

"What is it?" Lydia enquired.

"I have just remembered that the Earl will be in mourning for another three months."

"Of course!" Lydia exclaimed. "I had forgotten that too."

The Earl's mother, who had never been very strong and therefore was seldom seen at any social function, had died nine months ago.

She had long been bedridden and therefore her

passing had gone almost unnoticed, except formally in the social columns of the newspapers.

Thinking back now, Lydia remembered that her funeral had been private and had taken place in the small Church in the grounds of Royston Park.

Her father had not attended although he had instructed her to send a wreath.

It had been made up by the gardeners and a carriage had carried it to Royston Abbey early on the morning of the funeral.

Lydia had made the arrangements, then had not thought about it again.

Now she was aware that it would be considered incorrect for the Earl to marry until a year had passed.

That meant he could be married in April, as she said to her sister.

"A Spring bride! What could be more perfect!" Heloise exclaimed. "I must have a gown that makes everybody think of Spring, and if our family tiara is not big enough, I can borrow one of the Earl's. The Royston diamonds are famous!"

She drew in a deep breath as she said:

"They have whole sets each of sapphires, rubies and emeralds! Lady Burton was always talking about them and saying that any woman would give her right arm to possess such jewels!"

"You are so lovely that you have no need of a great number of diamonds," Lydia said.

"You must be mad!" Heloise contradicted. "One of the reasons why I want to marry the Earl is because his jewels are so marvellous."

It flashed through Lydia's mind that she herself would rather have his horses.

Then as if she could not prevent herself asking the question again she said:

"Are you sure you really love the Earl, Heloise? I feel certain that it would be impossible to be married to any man unless one loved him."

"You are talking utter nonsense!" Heloise snapped. "Quite frankly I think love and all that kissing and messing about is the sort of thing only servants do!"

"But . . . Heloise!" Lydia exclaimed in dismay.

She knew as she spoke that when she had heard about the Earl's love-affairs and married women spoke of him, there was a passionate look in their eyes.

She had even heard one of them say to another when she thought nobody else was listening:

"Hunter is a fantastic dream-lover! You have no idea how lucky I am!"

The words had been spoken in her father's house after dinner.

Because they were short-staffed Lydia had been carrying a coffee-cup from a side-table in the Drawing-Room where the footmen had overlooked it.

She was passing behind the sofa on which two ladies were sitting when she heard one of them mention the Earl.

Hearing the Earl's name always meant something to her because she was so interested in him. So she instinctively stopped to listen.

She was behind them and they had no idea she was there as the other lady replied:

"You are so lucky, Daisy. I have always thought the Earl is one of the most attractive men I have ever seen in my life, but alas, he has never looked in my direction."

"I would scratch your eyes out if he did!" Daisy answered. "I am crazily, wildly infatuated by him, and it is only with the greatest difficulty that I do not throw myself at his feet and beg him to run away with me."

"Daisy!"

The exclamation was horrified.

"How can you say such a thing! Think of the scandal it would cause! The Duke would undoubtedly call him out!"

"I doubt it!" Daisy replied. "Arthur must be well aware that Hunter has fought a dozen duels already, and has always been the winner."

She gave a little laugh that had a note of regret in it.

"Anyway, there is no fear of that! I am not so foolish as not to be aware that Hunter's *affaires de coeur* never last very long, and I doubt if any woman could hold him, once he is bored."

"I cannot imagine anybody being bored with you, Daisy!"

Daisy gave a deep sigh.

"Thank you, dearest. But while I am ecstatically happy to lie in the sun, I am well aware how quickly the weather can change."

"Then all I can say is," her friend replied, "that I envy you more than I can express in words, and I hope that the sunshine continues for a very, very long time."

"So do I," Daisy replied, "for I know that never again will I feel as I do now."

It was at that moment that the door of the room opened and the gentlemen joined the ladies.

Lydia hastily moved away from behind the sofa.

At the same time, she could not resist a little later looking for Daisy to find out who she was.

She then recognised her as her father's principal guest, the Duchess of Dorchester.

She was beautiful, there was no mistaking that.

Now looking back she remembered that she and her half-sister Heloise were not unalike, both having fair hair, blue eyes, and an exquisite complexion.

She was sure then that that was the type of woman the Earl most admired.

And yet she found it extraordinary, although she was too tactful to say so, that he should actually wish to marry Heloise.

"I suppose he must be in love with her," she told herself.

She thought however, although it might be unflattering to Heloise, that it was strange, when he had such a wide choice of other more sophisticated women.

"I will receive the Earl in the Drawing-Room," Heloise was saying, "and you had better arrange my hair a good deal better than you did last night."

"But you looked lovely last night!"

"Yes, when I started," Heloise agreed, "but half-way through the Ball it got loose and untidy. It was your fault for not making it more secure."

"If you danced the Lancers," Lydia said, "no hair-pins are strong enough to compete."

"Oh, do not argue!" Heloise said crossly. "I shall make certain that you do my hair properly for this afternoon, and I shall be wearing my new blue gown."

She paused before she said:

"He said to me last night when we were dancing that my eyes were exactly the colour of the sky, and he had thought of me when he was out riding."

"What did you answer?" Lydia asked curiously.

"I replied softly in the voice that always excites a man:

"'I am surprised that you should think of me, My Lord, but of course I am very, very flattered.'"

She mimicked her own voice as she spoke, and Lydia thought as she had often done before that Heloise was an excellent actress.

"What happened then?" she asked.

"His arms tightened around my waist and he said: 'You know how I feel about you?'

"And I replied: 'I have no idea, My Lord! You have never told me!'

"'Then I will tell you,' he answered, 'but not here. May I call on you tomorrow?'

"'I think that would be possible,' I replied a little doubtfully.

"'Make it possible!' he said. 'I have something important to say to you!'"

Heloise gave a little smile.

"I knew what that was, but I was far too clever to let him guess that I knew. I looked puzzled, and stared up at him with my eyes very wide and my lips parted. Suddenly he said:

"'If you look at me like that I shall kiss you here and now in the middle of the Ball-Room!'

"'Oh no!' I exclaimed, 'that would cause a scandal and Papa would be very angry!'

"'Then I shall wait until I see you tomorrow.'"

Lydia listened entranced. Then she said:

"I think that was very clever of you, Heloise. I am sure any other woman would have consented far too quickly, and it would be a mistake to forget that the Earl is called 'Hunter.'"

"I think that is a stupid name," Heloise remarked, "but I suppose it means that he likes to hunt."

"Yes, of course," Lydia agreed, "and if you had ever hunted you would know that it is disappointing to catch the fox too quickly."

Heloise thought about this for a moment. Then she said:

"When he asks me to marry him, I think I shall prevaricate a little, and say that I want time to make up my mind."

"That would be a clever idea," Lydia agreed.

"But suppose he then goes away?"

"I am quite sure," Lydia answered, "that this is the first time the Earl has ever asked anybody to marry him. He must love you, Heloise! Really love you! So you are very, very lucky!"

"Of course I am lucky," Heloise agreed. "I always have been. But I shall accept the Earl, just in case he changes his mind, and no decent man would back out of an engagement."

"If there is one thing of which you can be absolutely certain, it is that once the Earl of Royston has made up his mind, he will not change it," Lydia said.

"Anyway I shall take no chances," Heloise answered. "And that reminds me: I do not want anybody hovering about and interrupting us. I will tell Papa to stay in the Study and not to come barging in to talk about horses."

"I will arrange everything," Lydia said, "but you must expect Papa to come in for tea."

"I suppose he must," Heloise agreed, "but I do not want you!"

"No, of course not," Lydia said. "I will keep out of sight."

She felt a little pang of disappointment. She had so much wanted to meet the Earl.

Then she told herself that even if she was not allowed to talk to him, which was nothing unusual where a guest was concerned, at least it would not stop her from seeing him.

Having made all the arrangements she therefore waited at the top of the stairs and could see through the long high windows on either side of the front door the Earl's Chaise coming down the drive long before it reached the house.

It was drawn, as she expected, by two superbly matched horses, and as they swung round the court-yard to stop outside the front door she had her first glimpse of him.

He wore his top-hat at an angle on his dark head, and his coat fitted tightly over his broad shoulders.

She could see his face as he came through the front door and as she crouched down behind the banisters and peeped through them she looked at this strange, fascinating man as if she was seeing him for the first time.

There was undoubtedly a buccaneering look in his eyes and a faint twist to his lips, almost as if he mocked at himself as well as the world around him.

Then as the Butler took his hat and driving-gloves and went ahead of him across the Hall towards the

Drawing-Room Lydia thought it would be impossible for any man to look more distinguished, more masculine, more irresistibly attractive.

Only when she could no longer see him did she rise from her knees and know with a strange feeling within her breast that if she was honest the Earl attracted her in a manner that she could not explain.

Then she had the uncomfortable suspicion that what she was feeling for the first time was—love.

But as she walked upstairs to her bedroom she told herself she was being ridiculous.

How could she possibly feel love for a man to whom she had never spoken and been interested in only because he was a near neighbour?

But she knew it was more than that, and that although she had never admitted it, every day this winter when she had gone hunting she had hoped to see him.

And every time she had heard his name mentioned her heart had seemed to turn somersaults in her breast.

She ran to her room and walked across it to look at her reflection in the mirror.

What she saw were two large eyes with a worried expression in them which seemed to dominate her small pointed face that was actually a little too thin.

Her hair which was a strange indeterminate colour waved back naturally from her oval forehead, but because it had never seemed important Lydia did not arrange it in a fashionable manner, but because it was very long and thick merely twisted it into a chignon at the back of her head.

She supposed because she was like her mother that she had a certain prettiness, although it was not the flamboyant beauty of Heloise.

'Compared to her I am just a pencil-sketch to the brilliant colours of a Rembrandt or a Van Dyck,' she thought.

Then she laughed at her own fantasy.

It was true because in a way she knew from her position in her father's house there was something a little ghost-like about her.

She often thought she was like a shadow flitting along behind people who did not even notice her.

Then, as if she must console herself, she looked at the pile of books which stood beside her bed and on the shelves which she had ordered the estate carpenter to erect on either side of the fireplace.

While one side was packed with books, the other still had a few empty spaces left.

She either bought books, which meant sacrificing a gown she really needed, or else she purloined them from the Library downstairs, being certain that her father would not realise they were missing, and that Heloise never read a book anyway.

There they were, her companions, her inspiration, and most of all her consolation.

They consoled her for the fact that her mother was dead, her father did not like her, and Heloise was only concerned with her when she wanted something.

Because she had so much to do in running the house, she had no intimate friends outside and it was therefore the books that filled her life and saved her from being unhappy.

They carried her away to far distant lands, introduced her to people who were as real to her as anybody she had ever met, and gave her the feeling that she was searching for something which would some day fulfil the yearnings of her mind.

"Yes, I have my books," she murmured aloud.

She winced away from the thought that they were hardly to be compared with having the Earl.

The idea that he could ever be hers, even for the few minutes it took to waltz together, was so unthinkable that she laughed.

Downstairs he was proposing to Heloise, and it was understandable that he should want as his wife the most beautiful girl the London Season had ever seen.

Lydia thought that he must have come to the conclusion that it was time for him to marry, since in his position it was imperative that he should have an heir.

She thought too that because of the way he lived it was unlikely that he had ever had close contact with unmarried girls.

She was well aware that the Earl belonged to the smart 'Marlborough House Set' centring round the Prince of Wales who had already scandalised a great number of people by his interest in other women.

His beautiful Danish Wife, Princess Alexandra, was an object of general pity, but at the same time it was expected that a dashing man, especially a Royal Prince, should enjoy himself as he wished.

'I suppose Heloise will not mind if the Earl's interests are often elsewhere,' Lydia thought.

Then she knew that if she loved the Earl it would be an agony beyond words to know that he was no longer interested in her and that other women had taken her place even if only temporarily.

She knew that Heloise would not admit it, but her half-sister was not in love with anybody except herself.

If her pride was hurt by anything her husband did in the future, her heart would remain unaffected, if indeed she had a heart.

It was strange, Lydia thought looking back, how little affection Heloise had ever shown for anybody.

She certainly had not been fond of her mother and had found it increasingly boring to have to go to see her when she was ill.

Towards the end she had to be persuaded to do so by Lydia or Sir Robert.

"You have not been to see your mother for two days," Lydia had heard her father say on one occasion.

"I know, Papa, but I thought I had a slight cold," Heloise had replied, "and I knew it would be wrong to risk affecting Mama with it."

It was an excuse that was repeated too often for Sir Robert not to become suspicious.

"I do not want a lot of excuses," he had said finally. "You will go to see your mother every day, and that is an order!"

"Very well, Papa," Heloise agreed demurely.

When he had gone from the room she had stamped her foot and said petulantly to Lydia:

"What a bore Papa is! I cannot think why he does not leave me alone! He must realise if I were ill I would not want to see him."

"But he would want to see you, Heloise, because he loves you," Lydia said. "And I am sure your mother feels neglected, and that is unkind of you."

"I cannot help it," Heloise replied crossly. "You go and see her!"

"You are her daughter, and she loves you," Lydia protested.

"Well, I do not love her!" Heloise snapped. "People who are ill make me feel sick! I hate illness! I want to enjoy myself, and if Mama dies, that will stop me from doing so."

She ran out of the room with a defiant gesture, slamming the door behind her.

Lydia knew that her Stepmother was very hurt by her daughter's neglect, but although she tried to make Heloise more sympathetic she had no success.

Now as her thoughts went back to the Earl she wondered if he was like Heloise and had never really cared for anybody.

Was he without a heart? Was that the reason why he had broken so many and apparently been unaffected by the suffering of his victims?

'If that is true, then they are well suited to each other!' she thought.

At the same time, as she waited at the top of the stairs in order to watch the Earl leave, she hoped the servants were not aware of what she was doing.

Her father saw him to the front door, but Heloise remained behind in the Drawing-Room.

As they walked across the Hall and the Earl took his hat and gloves from the Butler, Sir Robert said:

"We will see you tomorrow, Royston, when we can go into further details of the trip. It certainly sounds extremely interesting."

"I hope you will think so," the Earl replied. "By

the way, I have a horse I would like to show you, a most amazing animal..."

Their voices died away as they walked down the steps to where the Earl's Chaise was waiting.

Lydia wondered what her father had meant about a 'trip.'

Because she was curious she ran down the stairs into the Drawing-Room.

Heloise was standing at the window looking out into the garden.

She turned as Lydia came into the room and threw out her arms.

"I am engaged! I am engaged!" she cried. "And we are to be married, but not until we return from some extraordinary place where the Earl insists on taking me."

"Where is that?" Lydia asked as she walked towards her.

"Honolulu!" Heloise answered. "And I have not the slightest idea where it is!"

chapter two

LYDIA could only stare at her sister in astonishment.

Then as her father came into the room she remembered that Honolulu was the capital of Hawaii—a group of islands in the Pacific Ocean.

She thought Heloise must have got it wrong, for it seemed impossible that the Earl of all people should want to go to such a strange, far-away part of the world.

But her father was able to explain the situation to them.

Two years previously King Kalakaua, he told them, had ascended the throne of Hawaii, and because he had a flourish and style which made him very different from all the previous Kings, he was determined to fashion his Kingship on the traditions of Western Monarchy.

He immediately began building himself a grand Palace and also planned a trip round the world which would make him the first Monarch to circumnavigate the globe.

"He organised gala horse-races, gave grand Balls and old-style Hawaiian feasts," Sir Robert related, "and entertained his many friends and visitors most extravagantly at the tax-payers' expense."

Lydia laughed.

"That is nothing new, Papa, where Monarchs are concerned!"

"It certainly earned the King the reputation of being Hawaii's 'Merry Monarch.'"

"Is that what he is?"

"Very much so," Sir Robert averred.

"He certainly sounds amusing," Lydia remarked. "But why should the Earl wish to visit him?"

"The King came to England on his world tour," Sir Robert explained, "and strange though it may seem, he charmed Queen Victoria with his British accent."

He paused before he went on:

"Her Majesty has therefore decided that she wishes to be represented at the King's Coronation which will take place in Honolulu in February."

"Now I understand," Lydia exclaimed. "How lovely for you, Heloise! You will have a special place at the Coronation, and I believe Honolulu is a very beautiful place."

"I shall certainly look forward to seeing it," Sir Robert said, "and I think the Coronation will have its amusing moments!"

There was so much more that Lydia wanted to hear about how they would travel to reach Honolulu, but

Sir Robert then left his daughters alone.

Heloise only wanted to talk about her clothes.

Because she could not help being curious Lydia asked after a little while:

"What did the Earl say when he proposed, Heloise?"

"I suppose it was romantic," her sister replied indifferently, "but I was so intent on making sure he really did ask me to marry him that it was not as dramatic as it should have been."

Lydia gave a little laugh.

"What did you expect? That the Earl would go down on one knee?"

"That has been done before," Heloise replied.

Lydia thought she could not imagine the Earl going down on his knees to anybody, least of all a young girl.

But she persisted in asking questions until at last Heloise said:

"Well, if you must know, he said: 'I want you to marry me. You are the most beautiful person I have ever seen, and I am sure we shall be very happy together.'"

"Is that all?" Lydia asked.

"It was enough," Heloise replied. "I said: 'Yes, I am sure we shall be happy.' Then he kissed me and said that he had to go to Honolulu and that he wanted me to go with him."

"With Papa!" Lydia added.

"Of course," Heloise agreed, "and the Earl did explain why we could not be married for another three months."

She looked a little petulant as she went on:

"I think it would have been more impressive if I could have gone with him as his Countess, but he said we could go to New York on the way, and he was sure that everybody there would think I was very beautiful."

"Of course they will!" Lydia agreed. "There is not likely to be any American girl as lovely as you."

"I have to think of my clothes, and quickly!" Heloise said. "We have very little time."

"When are you leaving?"

"Immediately after Christmas."

Lydia gave a cry of consternation.

"As soon as that? Oh, but of course! Papa said that the King was being crowned in February."

"I am not bothered about the King," Heloise exclaimed crossly. "I have to look sensational, so we must go to London immediately, Lydia, to choose at least part of my trousseau."

"The dressmakers will not be very keen to have to make a lot of things just before Christmas," Lydia said warningly.

"They will have to," Heloise insisted. "You know as well as I do, Lydia, that I have not nearly enough gowns even counting the ones I wore for my coming out in London. I am tired of them, anyway!"

Lydia remembered the money her father had spent on Heloise's Ball-gowns and the elaborate dresses she had for almost every hour of the day, and thought it was really quite unnecessary that she should want any more.

She knew however, that even to express such an idea would bring her sister's wrath down on her head, so she said nothing and merely began to make preparations for them to leave for London.

When Sir Robert heard what was planned he was annoyed.

"I have no wish to go to London just now," he said. "As it is, I am going to miss the horses while I am on this trip to the other side of the world."

"I will look after them, Papa," Lydia smiled.

"You will be unable to do that," Sir Robert replied, "because you are coming with us."

Lydia stared at him, not understanding. Then she said in a voice that did not sound like her own:

"Did you say that I am to ... come with you, Papa?"

"Has not Heloise told you?" Sir Robert asked. "Oh, I suppose she was not listening, but Royston said a battleship would be taking us from San Francisco to Honolulu."

Lydia was listening intently as he went on:

"He said it would be impossible for us to take a female servant on the ship who would upset the Crew. He therefore suggested that Heloise took on the journey instead of a lady's-maid, a companion who would be prepared to look after her and help her with her clothes."

"A companion!" Lydia repeated rather stupidly.

"It is quite obvious that will have to be you," Sir Robert said. "You are used to looking after Heloise, and you will keep her in good temper during any difficulties that are bound to arise at sea."

He paused before he added:

"Personally, I think it is a mistake for the Earl to insist on our accompanying him, but as he said, since he has just become engaged to Heloise, he has no wish to leave her behind."

"I can understand that, Papa," Lydia said. "At the same time, it seems a little strange for him to arrive not with a wife, which would be understandable, but with a *fiancée* and her father."

She did not mention her membership of the party knowing she would be kept very much in the background.

"I expect Royston has some very good reason of his own for this decision," Sir Robert answered.

The way her father spoke and the fact that he immediately changed the subject made Lydia suspicious.

From that moment she was quite certain in her own mind that the Earl had some ulterior reason for taking Heloise with him, apart from the fact that she was to be his wife.

It was something which she pondered and wondered about, but there were so many other things to occupy her mind that she had no time to think of anything but Heloise and her unceasing demands upon her time.

It was Lydia who took her sister to London and, while Heloise lay in bed resting, arranged for all the best dressmakers to come to her father's house at different hours.

It was Lydia who made it quite clear that either the gowns were completed in record time or else they would not be purchased.

It was Lydia who had to rush around to all the other shops finding shoes and gloves to match the gowns, bonnets that completed and complemented the morning and afternoon dresses which Heloise would be wearing.

She had to find a thousand-and-one other things, also, including sunshades, shawls, scarves and accessories which Heloise insisted must be new, as nothing she already had was good enough.

Sir Robert was a rich man and adored his beautiful daughter, but even he began to expostulate at her wild extravagance.

"I can hardly marry the Earl and let him be ashamed of me!" Heloise replied petulantly.

"He is not likely to be that," Sir Robert remarked. "At the same time, he will hardly expect you to take so much with you on the journey. Surely the majority of the things could wait until you return?"

"I am not going looking like a beggar-maid!" Heloise protested.

She began to get into one of her tantrums and Sir Robert hurriedly left the room leaving Lydia to soothe her sister down in a way that only she could manage to do, and to cancel one or two of the gowns that Heloise had ordered without her being aware of it.

At the same time, after five days in London Lydia began to think that any ship would sink under the weight of Heloise's trunks.

The fact that she looked ravishingly lovely in everything she put on certainly placated her father.

Lydia herself felt that no man, even the sophisticated Earl, would be able to resist anybody who looked so overwhelmingly beautiful as Heloise did when she was arrayed in her new gowns.

The Earl had not come to London as might have

been expected, because he preferred to be in the country, hunting and shooting.

"He is neglecting me!" Heloise complained. "I have a good mind to send him a note to say I want to see him immediately!"

"I think that would be a mistake," Lydia replied.

"I expected you would say that!" Heloise said rudely. "Why should you interfere?"

"I am not interfering," Lydia objected, "but you must realise that men love their sports, and as the weather is so perfect for hunting, you cannot expect the Earl to give it up just to be with you."

"I *do* expect him to!" Heloise said angrily.

Because she thought perhaps it was rather unnatural for a newly-engaged couple to be apart, Lydia had an idea.

"Why do you not go back to the country, Heloise?" she suggested. "I will fit the gowns for you. We are the same size, and any small alterations can be made at home by the sewing-woman."

Heloise thought about this for a moment. Then she said:

"That is a good idea! I am bored with fittings so I will go back to the country and you can stay here. But be as quick as possible! You must be home in two days' time because I shall want you to do my hair before the Christmas Ball."

"Yes, of course," Lydia agreed.

The Christmas Ball which was given, was an annual event which took place just before Christmas Day, given by the Lord Lieutenant.

He was a very old man, and everybody knew that when he either died or retired the Earl of Royston would be appointed to take his place.

Heloise was well aware of this and Lydia knew that her sister had every intention of making a dramatic appearance at the Ball, and would undoubtedly behave as if she was already the hostess.

"I will be back in time for the Ball," she promised, "and I expect you will want to wear one of your new gowns."

"That is a silly remark!" Heloise retorted scornfully. "I shall naturally wear the most sensational of them all which I think is the white lace with all the *diamanté* on it."

"I think so too," Lydia agreed, "and you will look like the Spirit of Winter!"

Heloise therefore returned to the country while Lydia stayed to find that trying to manage the fittings of all the dressmakers was more tiring than any day out hunting.

She was so exhausted by the time she got to bed that she fell asleep as soon as her head touched the pillow.

She had promised Heloise that she would be back the day of the Ball which meant she had to catch a very early train and was therefore called soon after six o'clock.

It was incorrect for her to travel alone, but Heloise had taken back with her the lady's-maid and one of the footmen who habitually travelled up and down to London.

Lydia therefore decided to travel alone, feeling it unnecessary to ask one of the older servants to accompany her.

She knew how much they disliked the trains which

they looked on as dangerous. So she went to the station alone, knowing her father would disapprove, but there was nothing else she could do.

She had arranged to have a reserved carriage and the Guard had locked her in when at the last moment the door was unlocked to allow a very elegant Lady, draped in the most expensive sables, to get into the carriage with her.

Lydia could see a lady's-maid on the platform carrying a jewel-case bearing a coronet on it before she got into another carriage.

The door was re-locked and the train set off.

Lydia looked at the newcomer with interest.

She was certainly very lovely and seemed to be of great importance, which made it strange that she should not have a carriage to herself.

Then as the train gathered speed the Lady said:

"I wonder if you would mind changing places with me? I feel ill if I sit with my back to the engine, and as the sun is on the other side of the compartment I do not wish it to be on my face."

There was very little sun and what there was was rather pale and watery but because her skin was very white and flawless, Lydia could understand her fears and replied:

"Yes, of course!"

After they had changed seats the Lady said:

"It is certainly unusual for me not to be travelling in a private train, or at least have a carriage to myself, but I only decided at the very last minute that I felt well enough to attend a Ball which is taking place tonight."

Lydia smiled.

"You must mean the Christmas Ball at the Marquess of Roehampton's house."

The Lady raised her eye-brows.

"Do you know him?"

"My father, who is Sir Robert Westbury, lives very near him."

The Lady stared at her. Then she said:

"Westbury? You are not saying—you cannot be the girl who is to marry the Earl of Royston?"

"That is my sister."

"Oh!"

For a moment it seemed there was nothing more to say. Then as if she felt she must talk the Lady said:

"I am the Countess of Milbourne and the Earl is a very old *friend* of mine."

The way she said it with a deliberate stress on the word 'friend' made Lydia think that the Countess had been more than friendly at one time with the Earl.

Then as if she could not prevent herself the Countess continued:

"It was certainly a shock and a surprise to everybody, especially the Earl's old friends, that he should become engaged, so precipitately and without any warning!"

"My sister is very beautiful."

Lydia thought as she spoke that the Countess, if she had not had herself strictly under control, would have snorted.

Instead she said:

"The Earl has always vowed he had no intention of marrying until he was very much older. Of course, your sister must have persuaded him to think otherwise."

There was certainly a spiteful sting in the Lady's words. Then she asked:

"How old is your sister?"

"She is eighteen."

"Oh, dear! I cannot help feeling sorry for the poor child! I am afraid the dear Earl, much as we all love him, will lead any woman, however experienced, however sophisticated, a dance once he is married! But a girl of eighteen . . . !"

She threw up her suede-gloved hands in horror and Lydia knew she was in fact, delighted that Heloise was so young and in consequence quite incapable of amusing the Earl and keeping him faithful.

It was an idea that had already gone through her mind.

Although she thought it extremely incorrect for the Countess to speak in such a manner because of her curiosity she could not help encouraging her.

"Do tell me about the Earl of Royston," she begged, "I have seen him many times, but I have actually never met him."

"You have never met him?" the Countess exclaimed. "Then I assure you, Miss Westbury, you are in for a surprise! He is different from other men, very, very different!"

"In what way?"

"I suppose, because he behaves as if he owns the world and everything in it, that one almost begins to believe it is true."

The Countess paused before she went on:

"In the case of other men that would make them conceited and pompous, but with the Earl it seems so natural to him to have everything his own way that we just give in and treat him as omnipotent."

She laughed as she spoke and it made her look very pretty.

At the same time there was a look in her eyes that was malicious, and Lydia knew she was longing to be spiteful, both about the Earl and his engagement.

"Have you known His Lordship for a very long time?" she asked.

"For years!" the Countess answered. "As I said, we are very old friends, so I shall be interested, very interested to meet your sister and find out what special attributes she has that have been so sadly lacking in all the other women who have in the past made themselves very much a part of Hunter's life."

The nickname slipped out by mistake, and immediately the Countess said firmly:

"Of course, as I have said, the Earl is a law unto himself, and therefore one cannot judge him by the same standards as one would judge other men."

Because she was fascinated and had never before been with somebody who knew the Earl and would talk to her about him, Lydia said very ingenuously:

"Another old friend of the Earl's was dining at my father's house the other night, the Duchess of Dorchester."

She saw by the expression in the Countess's eyes that the name was very familiar and almost as if the words came to her lips before she considered them she said:

"Of course—Daisy! That might well be the reason—I would not be at all surprised! I heard the Duke was furious and swearing revenge!"

She talked as if she was speaking to herself. Then

as she realized to whom she was talking, she said quickly:

"Oh, dear, I am talking nonsense! Yes, dear Daisy Dorchester is a friend of mine and of the Earl's. We all love her!"

She then began to talk of other things deliberately avoiding, Lydia was sure, any further mention of the Earl.

But Lydia had learned what she had wanted to find out, that it might be something to do with the Duchess of Dorchester which had made the Earl propose to Heloise so precipitately and without any warning.

She had thought it strange from the very beginning.

Heloise, while she had been a fellow-guest at parties with him and had of course been introduced, had never spoken about him as having danced with her, or as having sat next to her at dinner.

Had he done so, Lydia was quite certain she would have talked about him and boasted of her success.

When Heloise was in London during the Season every morning she had reiterated over and over again what a success she had been the night before, and had told Lydia of the compliments she had received and the names of the men who had paid them.

There had never been a mention of the Earl of Royston until suddenly out of the blue he was there, asking her to marry him.

'I wonder what really happened?' Lydia thought now and felt a little dismally that she would never know.

At the same time, ever since she had learned that she was to go to Honolulu with Heloise she had felt as though she was in a dream.

How could it be possible that she would at least be in the same party as the Earl, and even if he never spoke to her she could look at him and perhaps listen to him.

She had no idea, because her father did not know either, if they were to be just a party of four or if there would be a number of others with them travelling on the Queen's instructions.

'Perhaps Papa will know more now,' Lydia thought.

After she had said goodbye to the Countess and was driving home from the station in the carriage that was waiting for her, she found herself putting what she had heard about the Earl together.

Recalling what she had overheard at the dinner party, she realised now that it all fitted together like a jig-saw puzzle, and almost made a pattern.

She walked into the house to be told that her father wished to see her in the Study immediately upon her arrival.

Without even taking off her travelling-cape she hurried down the passage, wondering what could have happened.

She opened the door and her father looked up from the desk where he was writing to say sharply:

"You are back, and about time too!"

"What is the matter? What is wrong, Papa?"

Lydia pulled off her gloves as she spoke, then unclasped her fur-lined cape and put it down on one of the chairs.

"I did not say that anything was wrong!" Sir Robert replied. "It is just that your sister is impossible to manage when you are not here."

"I am sorry about that, Papa. What is the difficulty?"

"She keeps asking me to send for Royston as if he was a servant who must obey my command! The man is busy—of course he is busy at this time of the year! He is taking her to Honolulu with him. What more can she expect?"

"She came back from London because she wanted to see him."

"Well, I told her he is busy," Sir Robert said, "and Heloise's having hysterics about it, is not going to make him any more anxious to give up a day's hunting or shooting, to dance attendance on her!"

Lydia sat down on a chair beside the desk.

"Are you saying, Papa, that Heloise has not seen the Earl since she came home from London?"

"No, she has not! I told you, he is busy!" Sir Robert snapped.

Lydia could understand how annoying it must be for her sister, having returned especially to see the Earl to find there was nobody there to amuse her.

If she had stayed in London there would always have been admirers who could be invited to dinner or hostesses who would have been delighted to entertain her as the *fiancée* of the Earl of Royston.

She knew how difficult Heloise could be in such circumstances, and taking her cape and gloves from the chair she said:

"I will go and talk to Heloise, Papa. I presume she will see the Earl tonight as you are dining with the Marquess before the Ball?"

"Of course she will see him!" Sir Robert said. "And you had better tell her not to make a scene. Royston will not stand for any woman ranting at him—I am quite certain of that!"

Lydia was certain of it too.

She went upstairs to her sister's bedroom and found her resting.

She was looking exquisitely beautiful with her hair which had been washed earlier in the day falling over her shoulders, and wearing a negligée.

She was lying on a *chaise longue* in front of the fire, an ermine rug over her legs.

"So you are back!" she said in the same aggressive tone that her father had used. "I wasted my time coming home. I might just as well have stayed in London with you."

"You would have found it very tiring," Lydia replied. "I must have had nearly a hundred fittings on your behalf, but the gowns are lovely!"

"What is the point of having lovely gowns with nobody to admire them?" Heloise pouted.

"I have brought the white lace with me and it looks absolutely wonderful!" Lydia said. "If you wear your mother's diamond necklace with it you will undoubtedly be the best dressed and loveliest woman in the Ball room!"

"I shall be very angry if I am anything else!" Heloise replied sulkily.

Lydia looked at the clock.

"You should have your bath in another hour-and-a-half," she said. "I will just go and take off my bonnet and be ready to do your hair."

As she walked along to her own bedroom she thought she was very tired and what she would really like was a cup of tea.

She found one of the housemaids unpacking her trunk and asked her to order it from the kitchen.

She then sat down in front of her mirror, thinking it was a good thing that she was not going to the Ball tonight.

"I would be much too tired to enjoy myself," she told her reflection.

Then she wondered if that was true.

She was tired of being fitted for gowns she would never wear, tired of trying to keep her sister in a good mood.

If only she could be allowed just for once to be herself, to be an individual, who was not just a shadow in her sister's life, she was sure she could enjoy herself.

Then almost as if the sun was shining through the window or the lights all suddenly came on at once, she remembered she was going to travel across the world to an exotic land.

And she would be accompanying, whether he was aware of it or not, the Earl of Royston.

The following day Heloise when she awoke was all smiles.

It was not difficult for Lydia to know that the Earl had been charming and very apologetic for being so neglectful.

"He said he had thought that I was going to be in London until yesterday," Heloise said, "and as he was going away so soon he had planned every minute of his time and would have found it difficult to make so many cancellations, even though he was longing to see me."

Lydia smiled to herself and thought the Earl had certainly been very tactful.

Her father too told her that the Ball had been a great success.

"Your sister outshone everybody!" he said proudly. "There was no doubt that Royston thought so too."

"I am glad about that, Papa."

"She cannot expect him to follow her about like a tame poodle," Sir Robert growled. "Not his style at all! You had better put some sense into her head before she gets married."

"I will do my best, Papa," Lydia replied, "but Heloise feels she had a right to a great deal of his attention."

"Of course! Of course!" Sir Robert agreed. "The trouble is that Royston has had too much attention himself in the past!"

"I met a lady on the train," Lydia said, "who told me she knew him very well. She was the Countess of Milbourne."

Sir Robert laughed.

"She certainly knows him *very* well!" he said with a note in his voice that conveyed far more than his actual words.

Then his mood changed and he said angrily:

"You do not want to go chit-chatting to other women about Royston, and certainly not to repeat anything you hear to your sister. Do you understand?"

"Yes, of course I understand, Papa, and I would not think of doing anything unkind. But Heloise can be very demanding."

Sir Robert knew this was true and as if he had no solution to the problem he merely said ominously:

"Keep her away from women like the Countess, and that is an order where you also are concerned!"

Lydia did not bother to say that she was never likely to meet the Countess or any of the other social personalities who were friends with the Earl, except in unusual circumstances.

Then she remembered that if she was to travel with her sister and her father to Hawaii, that would certainly be 'unusual circumstances.'

There was however so much to do over Christmas and so many arrangements to be made before they could leave in early January that Lydia had no time to think of her own social problems.

She had to plan for Heloise's gowns, trunks, bonnet-boxes, and Heloise herself.

It was only at the last minute that she realised she had had no time to think of what she herself should wear on the trip and that she had not even considered what would be necessary for her to pack.

It was fortunate that she could wear some of Heloise's old clothes, and there were a number of summer dresses that her sister would never look at again and which she thought had been thrown away.

There were also several evening gowns she did not like and which she refused to wear.

Lydia picked out the most simple of them and had the seamstress in the house remove some of the decoration from the evening-gowns.

She not only knew that she must in no way try to attract attention to herself, but she was also aware because she was, as she admitted, a shadowy figure, she looked best in things that were very simple.

This meant gowns made either in white or the soft pastel shades which as a general rule did not particularly suit Heloise.

She preferred to wear the bright blue of her eyes, the pink of her cheeks or white evening gowns which were elaborately embroidered with *diamanté* or decorated with flowers.

She also wore gowns ornamented with feathers or row upon row of expensive lace.

Because Lydia seldom appeared at any of the social parties in the neighbourhood and only occasionally at those which took place in her father's house, she had very few gowns of her own.

Those she had were home-made or else had been discarded by Heloise and re-fashioned to suit her by the seamstress.

"I shall certainly look like the beggar-maid at His Majesty's Court!" Lydia told herself remembering what Heloise had said.

Then she thought it was very unlikely that she would attend the Coronation as her sister would do, but perhaps would be able to see it by standing in the crowd.

At any rate nobody could prevent her from seeing Hawaii, and whenever she had a minute to herself she ran to the Library to thumb through the Encyclopaedias for references and looked daily along the crowded bookshelves for anything which might tell her more about the islands.

All she could find out was that they had been discovered by Captain Cook who, while at first he had been given an overwhelming welcome, was later killed by the Hawaiian warriors.

The bones of the greatest navigator in the world had been scattered so that it had been impossible to find and bury them all completely.

This had all happened a century ago, and by all accounts Hawaii which was an independent native Kingdom, was now very friendly towards the British, although the Americans were encroaching upon the islands, determined to annexe their territory to their own country.

Lydia stored everything she learned about Hawaii in her mind, only wishing she had more time and when she was in London could have visited the British Museum, or perhaps one of the big Libraries to find out more.

'There must be somebody who can tell me about them,' she thought despairingly.

As if somebody had whispered the answer to her, she suddenly knew that the person who would undoubtedly know more about them than anybody else would be the Earl.

It was only the day before they were actually leaving that the Earl came to the house to make the last-minute arrangements with her father.

"If he is coming here I want to see him alone," Heloise said, "so do not monopolise him, Papa! You know that once you start talking about horses it is impossible for anybody else to get a word in edgeways!"

She spoke in an impertinent manner which always made Lydia feel uncomfortable, and Sir Robert said sharply:

"He says in the note he sent me that he wants to talk about the journey. You will have plenty of time with eight days on the ship across the Atlantic, and God knows how many in the train across America, to talk your head off!"

Heloise suddenly veered round like a weather-vane and said plaintively:

"I have no wish to travel all that way! Why can we not stay at home and get married?"

"You will do that when you return," Lydia said, "and you know you want a Spring wedding with your bridesmaids all carrying Spring flowers."

"I have changed my mind," Heloise said. "I think it would be far more appropriate to carry orchids."

"They are not so colourful," Lydia answered, "but we can talk about it on the trip."

She felt with a little throb of her heart that it was unlikely her sister would talk about anything else except her wedding, and it would therefore be difficult to twist the conversation round to the subjects she wanted to learn about.

About America, of which she knew very little, and of course, especially about Hawaii.

Already she was seeing it in her mind's eye as an El Dorado of sunshine, palm-trees, a blue sea with waves breaking on golden sands, and the vivid colours of the flowers.

All this she felt would make it seem like a fairy-tale land.

"I am so lucky, so very, very lucky," she told herself.

She found it hard to believe, after being pushed into the background for so long and told by Heloise not to appear unless it was absolutely necessary, that she was actually to go with her on this fascinating journey.

Heloise, she soon learnt was not at all pleased by the idea.

"I cannot think why I could not have my lady's-maid with me," she complained. "It is quite ridiculous to suggest that Jones would make trouble on the ship with the sailors. She is too old, for one thing!"

"It is very exciting for me to be able to come in her place," Lydia said, "and you know, if you are honest, that I can do your hair far better than Jones can!"

"Well, you are not to push yourself forward, just because you are my sister," Heloise warned crossly. "I do not want another woman with me. I would have much preferred to be the only one."

Lydia stared at her for a moment before she said:

"Are there to be no other members of the party except you and Papa?"

"No, of course not!" Heloise said. "The Earl said it was his idea that I should go with him when the Queen asked him to represent her at the King's Coronation, because he was frightened that in his absence I might fall in love with somebody else."

She preened herself a little before she went on:

"It was quite intelligent of him to think that because it is something which might easily happen."

Lydia laughed.

"I cannot believe anybody more important than the Earl would pop down the chimney the moment he had gone away!"

"One never knows!" Heloise said mysteriously.

"You told me that the Earl was the most important man in England!"

"Well, in a way he is," Heloise admitted. "None of the Dukes or Marquesses have more money than he has or finer houses. Papa says his race-horses are supreme!"

"Then I think it is a very good thing that you are going with him to Honolulu," Lydia said. "Just supposing he thought that one of the dancing-girls in their grass skirts and with hibiscus flowers in their hair was even more beautiful than you! He might marry her, then where would you be?"

Lydia was only teasing, but Heloise gave a scream of anger.

"How can you suggest anything so degrading?" she cried furiously. "Dancing girls cannot be compared to me! They are immoral creatures who set out to attract men, and they certainly would not expect to marry an English nobleman!"

Lydia laughed.

"I was not being serious, Heloise," she said. "At the same time, you must be aware that the Earl is a very attractive man, and wherever he goes there will always be women running after him and ready to entice him if they get the chance."

She spoke quite seriously because although she did not want to upset her sister she thought it would be a mistake for her to be too complacent.

She should not expect the Earl, because he was in

51

love with her, not to need the consideration and flattery which she was sure every man needed, and he especially.

Heloise tossed her head.

"He will not find anybody as beautiful as me," she said, "in fact he has already said that I am the most beautiful girl he has ever seen."

Lydia gave a little sigh. She thought it would be impossible to make Heloise understand that, unless she was very much mistaken, her beauty would not content somebody like the Earl for ever.

She did not know why she was so sure he would want more from a woman than a beautiful face, but she had the feeling that he was seeking for something deeper, not only from women but from life.

Something which cynically he was almost certain he would never find.

Then she shook herself.

"I am just imagining all these things about him because he is so handsome."

Then she knew that when she had watched him through the banisters coming into the house, she had felt in some strange way that her instinct told her things about him almost as if he was talking to her.

It was something she could not explain, and yet it was there.

It was so vivid and everything she heard about him added to her knowledge of him.

"Tomorrow I shall be near him," she whispered.

She felt as if there was a lark singing in the sky.

chapter three

"THIS is my daughter Lydia," Sir Robert said.

"Your daughter?" the Earl exclaimed in surprise.

As he held out his hand Lydia realised that neither her father nor Heloise had told him that she was coming with them on the journey.

In fact, he had been expecting a paid companion or perhaps a poor relation who would be grateful for the privilege.

'That is exactly what I am!' Lydia thought with a wry smile.

Then as the Earl's hand touched hers she knew that to meet him was what she had been longing for, and she felt as if she vibrated to his strength and his attraction.

"I hope you will enjoy the voyage, Miss Westbury," he was saying.

As he spoke the conventional words she was aware that his eyes were looking at her, taking in every detail of her appearance.

In some strange way she could not explain he seemed to be looking deeper as if, as she had thought before, he was seeking for something which he thought he would never find.

"It is very wonderful for me to be included on such an adventurous journey," Lydia said demurely.

Simple enough words, but sharply, as if she thought she was imposing on the Earl, Heloise said:

"Lydia, my bracelet is undone. Do it up."

Quickly Lydia moved to her sister's side where she was already seated comfortably in an armchair in the Drawing-Room section of the private coach that was attached to the train which was carrying them to Liverpool.

She was not surprised to find that the Earl had his own railway coach which he used whenever he travelled any distance.

She was well aware that many of the rich noblemen had not only their own railway carriages, but even their own trains.

It was something she had never travelled in before, and once they started off she looked around her in delight.

There were the Earl's servants wearing his livery to bring them first coffee or drinks, then as the day progressed there was luncheon, tea, and a light dinner before they finally arrived at Liverpool.

It was usual, Lydia learnt for the Atlantic Liners to sail at midnight.

The passengers boarded earlier, unpacked and prepared themselves for what, at this time of the year, everybody anticipated would be a rough crossing.

Heloise had already been working herself up into a frenzy in case she should be seasick.

"Even if you are, nobody will see you, except of course, me," Lydia said consolingly.

"It sounds so horrid and so common to be sick," Heloise said. "Oh, why could we not stay at home? I have no wish to go to Honolulu or any other such outlandish place!"

She had said this so often in the days before they were to leave that Lydia became afraid in case she refused to go at the last moment, which meant that she too would have to stay behind.

But when Heloise broached the idea to Sir Robert he was quite firm.

"We have agreed to go and you cannot back out now," he said. "Besides, you will look very silly if the Earl, while he is away, regrets having become engaged to you and wants to break it off."

"I am quite certain he will not do that," Heloise said.

At the same time Lydia thought her father had spoken so positively that Heloise was compelled to admit, if only to herself, that it might be a possibility.

At any rate she resigned herself with a very bad grace, being more than usually rude and disagreeable to Lydia until they had reached London where the Earl was waiting for them.

Lydia effaced herself as much as she could on the journey North.

She sat in a far corner of the Drawing-Room and was delighted to find that every newspaper and practically every published magazine was provided by the Earl for his guests.

Even while she appeared to be turning over the pages and reading she was really watching him, thinking that now she was close to him he was even more attractive than he had seemed at a distance.

She found it difficult to analyse what it was that made him so different from other men.

Then she thought that one of the most attractive things she had ever seen in a man was the way his eyes twinkled when something really amused him.

At other times he would look bored and, she thought, cynical, but when he was laughing his eyes laughed too.

She found herself waiting to see his face change.

By the time the long train journey was over and they were boarding the Cunard Steamship *Etruria* she knew that she was hopelessly captivated by a man who was never likely to notice her existence or to realise that she was anything but a shadow of her sister.

"I must be content to count my blessings," Lydia told herself.

She found when she got aboard that they were quite considerable.

She had learned because she read the newspapers that the largest ships designed by Sir William Cunard were the *Umbria* and the *Etruria*.

They carried three masts and enough sail to continue their passage should the mechanical power fail.

They were the first of the large ships that could

cross the Atlantic in eight days and were different in every way from their predecessors.

"Thank goodness," Lydia heard her father saying, "the passenger cabins have, at last, been placed amid-ships where the pitching is the least noticeable. When I have travelled before it was certainly in very different conditions from this."

He looked round as he spoke at the comfortable Stateroom which was heated by steam and lit by gas.

Because the Earl was of such importance and could certainly afford to pay for what he required there was one of the best cabins for each of his guests, and one had been converted into a Sitting-Room.

This was filled with hot-house flowers from his greenhouses at Royston Abbey, and Lydia also no-ticed there was every newspaper and magazine avail-able, a large box of chocolates, another of marron glacés, and also a box of her father's favourite cigars.

'We shall certainly be comfortable,' she thought with a smile.

As she spoke she heard Heloise's voice calling her from her cabin.

"Come and help me, Lydia!"

When her sister joined her she said sharply:

"There is no reason for you to be hanging about with us. When you are not attending to me you can sit in your own cabin!"

Lydia meekly agreed and when she found her most comfortable cabin which was next door to her sister's, she knew it would be no hardship.

She was quite certain that if Heloise had had any-thing to do with it she would have been relegated to one of the inside cabins on the other side of the corridor which were meant for lady's-maids and valets and which had no port-holes and no view of the sea.

She would have liked to thank the Earl for treating her so well, but thought that would certainly seem embarrassing, especially as he would not have expected the companion to be Heloise's sister.

As they were so late coming aboard, Heloise decided to go to bed immediately.

Lydia unpacked for her, finding, as she might have expected, that there was not enough room in her cabin for all the things she had brought and they therefore overflowed into hers.

As she had so few things of her own this constituted no difficulty, and anyway by the time Heloise had finished with her she was too tired to unpack her own things and decided to leave it for the morning.

Heloise wanted some water to drink in case she was thirsty during the night, and Lydia went to the Sitting-Room to see if there was any there.

She found there, as she expected, a tray containing ship decanters with broad flat bottoms filled with brandy and whisky, and also a syphon of soda water.

She was just wondering whether to take the whole soda syphon to Heloise when the door opened and the Earl came in.

She had not expected to see him, thinking he would very likely have gone with her father to the Smoking-Room which was, she had heard, where the gentlemen on board met to drink and play cards.

She was quite sure that was where her father would be, because he would be curious to find out who would be travelling to America with them.

The Earl had changed from the tweed suit he had been wearing on the train into a yachting jacket with brass buttons that she was sure he wore when he was on his own yacht.

It made him look even more like a buccaneer or a pirate than usual, though there was no genuine or obvious reason for thinking so, except perhaps for the look in his eyes which was what she expected to see when he was at sea.

"What can I get for you, Miss Westbury?" he asked.

Because she was looking at him and thinking of him, for a moment Lydia found it hard to understand what he had asked her.

Then she was conscious that because she had been so busy unpacking for Heloise her hair was a little untidy and her gown creased.

Only as she put up her hand to smoothe down her hair did she answer:

"Heloise required something to drink and I was just wondering whether I could take her the whole syphon."

"I think I can afford to order another one."

His eyes were twinkling and she thought he was laughing at her.

"I must sound very stupid," she said, "but there has been so much to do these last few days that I am finding it hard to think straight."

"I expect the truth is that you are tired," the Earl remarked, "and I also have the idea that you are excited."

"Why should you think that?"

"I noticed in the train that you were looking out

of the window almost as if you were afraid of missing something."

Because what he said was so unexpected Lydia could only stare at him before she replied:

"I have never been as far North as this before, and I did find the countryside unusual, and yet in a way it was what I expected."

"And what are you expecting to find across the Atlantic?"

"A very, very large Continent called 'America'!"

The Earl laughed.

"You are right, it is very large, and we have to go, as you already know, from one side of it to the other before we can embark again for our final destination."

The way he spoke made Lydia clasp her hands together as she said:

"It is difficult for me to express how thrilled I am by the thought of travelling so far and most of all seeing Hawaii."

"Why, particularly?" he enquired.

"I think because even the little I have read has made it sound like a dream place, quite unreal, which could exist only in one's imagination."

"I only hope that it lives up to your expectations," the Earl said. "Most places and people are disappointing on closer acquaintance!"

"I am sure that is not true," Lydia replied. "Please do not disillusion me before I actually get there!"

The Earl laughed again.

"I will not do that, for in fact I too am much looking forward to seeing Honolulu."

Lydia smiled at him, then remembered that Heloise

would be very angry that she had been away for so long.

She picked up the soda-water syphon saying:

"Thank you for letting me take this to my sister."

She turned round to return to Heloise but before she reached the door the Earl asked:

"Why have I not seen you before?"

"You may not have seen me, My Lord," Lydia replied, "but I have seen you very frequently."

"You have?" he exclaimed in surprise. "Where?"

"In the hunting-field," Lydia answered, "and I admire your horses more than I can possibly express."

"And, I hope, their rider?"

The way he asked the question made Lydia give a little laugh.

"I cannot imagine that you expect me to add my plaudits to those you have received already in such abundance."

She swept through the door before he could reply, and only as she saw her sister lying in bed waiting for her did she ask herself how she could have been so imprudent as to speak to the Earl in such a manner.

Heloise certainly would be angry and even her father might have disapproved.

Then she knew the magnetism she had sensed in the Earl when she had seen him by peeping through the bannisters was, when she was close to him, so strong that it made her feel exhilarated.

It was difficult to explain in words, and yet she remembered hearing once a very old man reminiscing about the great Duke of Wellington, and he had said:

"Whenever Wellington came into a room the tempo

rose and everybody sat up and seemed to come alive."

That, Lydia thought, was exactly the quality the Earl had.

Because he teased her, or just before he was there, she felt the tempo rise and she became exhilarated almost as if she had drunk a glass of champagne and it had gone to her head.

"You have been a long time!" Heloise said crossly.

"I had to find a syphon for you," Lydia replied. "I expect there will be other mineral waters tomorrow, or perhaps you prefer lemonade? But there is soda-water tonight, and I know it would be a mistake to drink out of the taps in your basin."

"I know that!" Heloise snapped. "I can assure you, Lydia, I am not taking any chances of upsetting myself any more than the sea will do."

"Now try to sleep," Lydia begged, "and you will soon get your 'sea legs.'"

Heloise drank a little of the soda-water, then lay back against the pillows.

There were several things she wanted fetched and put beside her before finally Lydia was able to get away to her own cabin.

Now she did not feel as tired as before, and she thought of the Earl all the time she was undressing.

When finally she got into bed it was quite a long time before she fell asleep.

The next three days were a misery.

Almost before they were out of harbour and crossing the Irish Sea the ship began to pitch and roll and by the time they reached the Atlantic it was very rough indeed.

Heloise made such a fuss about being sea-sick that after twenty-four hours of her moaning and groaning and repeating over and over again that she would rather be dead, than endure any more, Lydia sent for the ship's doctor.

Because he was a man Heloise made an effort to be charming to him, and as he was obviously bowled over by her beauty he called half-a-dozen times a day to see if there was anything he could do to alleviate her suffering.

Finally, he gave her a sedative which made her sleep, and almost worn out with having been at her side both by day and by night, Lydia found for the first time that she had a few minutes to herself.

Despite the fact that the sea was very rough she knew she must have some air.

She felt stifled in the cabin and knew however cold and unpleasant it might be outside it would at least be better than listening to Heloise's complaints.

She put on her thickest clothes and her tweed overcoat which she had worn in the country.

She was aware it would be quite impossible to keep any sort of bonnet on her head, so she put a chiffon scarf over her hair and tied it in a bow under her chin.

Walking unsteadily because the ship was heaving very uncomfortably she found her way onto the Promenade Deck which was wisely divided with a railing from those who were brave enough to sit outside in deck-chairs.

There were several men walking round the ship and even they looked a little 'green about the gills,' but there were no women.

Lydia, because she never had time to think about

herself, was not aware that they looked at her in surprise and then in admiration as she started to walk along the Deck.

Despite the waves that occasionally splashed over the side and the wind which seemed to be howling overhead like a banshee, the sea looked magnificent with white crested waves which reminded her of the fairy stories she had read as a child.

She had been told then that the waves were the horses of the Princes of the sea, and she believed in them as she believed in mermaids and the water-nymphs who lurked in streams and lakes and could be seen resting on the banks only at dawn and dusk.

She was thinking of this when she heard somebody beside her say:

"You are very adventurous, Miss Westbury! I did not expect to find you braving the weather. But perhaps you are an experienced sailor?"

Lydia turned her head to find the Earl was standing beside her and she replied:

"How could anything be so magnificent? I am expecting Neptune at any moment to rise up in all his majesty, his trident in his hand."

The Earl laughed.

"I am afraid I cannot offer you anything so Royal until we reach Hawaii, but you will be meeting the richest man in America when you get to New York."

"Do you mean Mr. Vanderbilt?" Lydia enquired.

"Of course, but I am surprised you should be aware of whom I meant."

Lydia thought it was slightly insulting that he should think her so ignorant.

Then she knew that had he been talking to Heloise

"I think it would be impossible to find anybody more beautiful!" Lydia agreed.

It flashed through her mind as she spoke that Lydia and the Duchess of Dorchester were very alike, and she had almost added that she knew Heloise was the type the Earl admired.

Then to her astonishment he said as if he read her thoughts:

"You are right, but there are of course, exceptions to every rule."

She turned again to look at him, her eyes very wide.

"How could you know what I was thinking?"

"I have just asked myself the same question."

Lydia looked down.

"It is . . . something you must . . . not do."

"But suppose I cannot help it?"

"Then, as I have already said, My Lord, you need not concern yourself with me. I am used to being unnoticed, and perhaps now I should go below. Heloise may want me."

She would have walked away from him but the Earl said:

"It is always a mistake to run away from the unexpected or to be afraid."

Lydia held onto the ship's rail with both hands.

"I am not afraid," she said in a low voice.

"I think that is untrue," the Earl replied. "We are all a little afraid of the unknown, but it could be very exciting and very enjoyable to explore and find out what for the moment we cannot completely understand."

She thought he was still talking of the way he had

been able to read her thoughts.

There were a million questions she wanted to ask him and she knew that what was happening now was the most fascinating experience of her whole life.

She knew she ought to make some excuse to leave him, for both Heloise and her father would disapprove of what they would think of as her monopolising the Earl, but she could not bring herself to go.

She was afraid that once they reached New York and Heloise was herself again she might never have another chance of talking to him.

"You said you had seen me in the hunting-field," he said. "Do you enjoy hunting?"

"It is what I look forward to as the only exciting thing which ever happens to me," Lydia replied.

"I think you should add to that: 'Up until now,'" the Earl remarked.

"Apart from the journey, do you think there are other exciting things for me to discover?" Lydia asked.

"But of course!" he replied. "You are very young, and I am sure you have not really begun to live."

That was true, Lydia thought.

When she remembered her life at home and the household duties that occupied her time, the books that were her only companions, she knew exactly what the Earl meant and it was something she had missed so far.

"If nothing else ever happens in the future," she said impulsively, "I shall at least have this to remember."

She was looking at the sea, but she knew it was not only the voyage or the place they were going to that she would remember, but being with the Earl.

"Then enjoy every moment of it," he said quietly, "and do not let mistaken ideas of duty or pride prevent you from reaching out towards your dream."

She was so surprised at what he said and the way he spoke that she turned to look at him.

He was nearer than she expected and his eyes were looking into hers.

For a moment they just looked at each other. Then as the spray from a wave breaking against the side of the ship made them both stiffen Lydia came back to reality.

Without saying anything she walked away and left the Earl alone at the railing.

It was not until two days before they were due to reach New York that Heloise felt well enough to leave her bed.

This had meant that Lydia had not been able to take her meals in the Dining-Room but had them brought to Heloise's cabin by the stewards.

She was disappointed because never again had she had a conversation with the Earl.

Although she had hoped to see him when she went on the Promenade Deck very early in the morning before Heloise was awake, and sometimes in the afternoons when she was asleep, he was never there.

She wondered if she had offended him, or even shocked him, by the way she had talked so openly.

And yet she knew every word was something that she would remember and recite over and over again to herself when she was alone.

Sir Robert told her that the Earl had been invited up onto the bridge by the Captain and as he was a keen yachtsman he was enjoying watching them navigate the Liner.

She knew also that the Earl exercised regularly in the Gymnasium, which was a new facility in the ship.

Now they were in smoother waters he played Deck-Tennis with some of the other passengers, not surprisingly being so good at it that he always emerged the victor.

"We have some excellent Bridge in the evening," Sir Robert said, "which would certainly not amuse you girls. But there is a Band, and one or two of the passengers have been well enough to dance."

As he said this Heloise roused herself from the lethargy she had been in ever since she had been sea-sick.

"Are you telling me, Papa, that Hunter is dancing with other women?"

"No, of course not," Sir Robert said, "but I am sure it is something he would want to do if you would take the trouble to get up and dress!"

"I do not like the sea!" Heloise said plaintively.

"It is something you will have to get used to," Sir Robert replied. "Your future husband is very pleased with his new yacht, so there is every likelihood of his visiting the Mediterranean later on in the summer."

He walked out of the cabin as he spoke and Heloise asked Lydia:

"Why did you not tell me that they were dancing?"

"How would I know that?" Lydia countered. "I have been here with you, as you well know!"

"I shall come down to dinner tonight," Heloise decided.

"I am quite certain you will no longer feel sick,"

Lydia said, "and you could have got up yesterday or even the day before if you had wished to. The Doctor says that even people who are very sea-sick usually recover after two or three days."

"It is your fault for not persuading me," Heloise said crossly.

She went down to dinner the last two nights but Lydia stayed in her cabin.

She wanted desperately to see the Earl again.

Yet because he now meant so much more to her than he had before she had met him, she knew it would hurt her to watch him paying court to Heloise.

He was doubtless looking at her with the admiration that always filled every man's eyes when they looked at her sister's beautiful face.

"I cannot bear it!" Lydia told herself, then was ashamed that she could be so foolish.

When the liner docked in New York, not only were they met by the Couriers arranged by the Earl, but also Mr. Vanderbilt had sent his secretary with two carriages to convey them to his house where they were to stay.

Lydia had not realised until now that they were to be his guests and she was surprised that her father had not mentioned it to her.

However she had had few private conversations with him except when he came to see Heloise.

Now she tried to remember all she had heard about the Vanderbilts and their millions.

She found it fascinating to think that for the first time in her life she was meeting people she had only read about in the newspapers and never thought she would actually see in the flesh.

Vaguely at the back of her mind she remembered reading of the famous Commodore, the Railroad King of America who had built up a huge fortune.

He had the vision of linking the Atlantic and the Pacific by his Railroads.

Now he was dead, but his son who had inherited his great wealth was to be their host.

"Vanderbilt certainly does things in style!" Sir Robert said to the Earl as they drove in an extremely comfortable carriage drawn by four horses, away from the dock.

"Wait until you see his house!" the Earl replied.

"Is it very unusual?" Sir Robert asked.

"After his father the Commodore died in 1877," the Earl replied, "William Henry, the President of the New York Central, realised he was the richest man in the world and decided to build himself a Royal Palace."

Sir Robert laughed and the Earl went on:

"His designers suggested building it of marble, as the highest expression of power, but Vanderbilt was afraid of marble and believed evil eyes dwelt in its cool shine."

Sir Robert looked surprised, but Lydia was listening intently.

"He was superstitious," the Earl went on, "and with reason since two millionaires, one of them an Astor, died soon after their mansions of marble had been built."

"How extraordinary!" Sir Robert exclaimed. "So what did Vanderbilt choose?"

"He ordered instead three massive brownstone

houses," the Earl explained, "one for himself, and one for each of his two daughters."

By the time they reached the brownstone house Lydia was filled with curiosity as to what it would be like.

She had expected something on the same lines as the grand houses in Park Lane, one of which belonged to the Earl.

Instead she found a conglomeration of priceless treasures put together like a patchwork of opulence which gave them a nightmare quality.

The house itself was overwhelming with doorways as majestic as triumphal arches and gilded ceilings curved like sections of Egyptian Mummy cases.

On the floors were rugs smothering rugs, on the walls pictures almost overlapping pictures, and every bit of space in the house covered with lamps, vases, figurines, *objets d'art* of every sort and description.

Each piece worth a fortune, was eclipsed by the next piece, until it was impossible to look at and admire anything without being distracted by something else.

It was perhaps because their hostess, Mrs. William Vanderbilt, was as overwhelming as the house that the Earl decided they should not stay more than one night, but would leave the next day for San Francisco.

Mrs. Vanderbilt was disappointed, to put it mildly.

She was socially wildly ambitious, an energetic unhappily married woman who had no other outlet to distract her.

She had obviously looked forward to presenting the Earl to the other social climbers in New York and had arranged not only a huge dinner-party for the night they arrived, but also a Fancy-dress Ball the night after.

Heloise was disappointed but the Earl was adamant.

"If there is one thing which will not wait for us," he said, "it is the King's Coronation!"

Even Mrs. Vanderbilt had to agree to this.

She had entertained King Kalakaua when he had been the first Monarch ever to dazzle America, and she played with the idea of accompanying them to Honolulu.

Fortunately the Earl with great tact was able to dissuade her by saying that as she had not received an invitation to the Coronation, it might, if she turned up unexpectedly, be embarrassing.

When they left the overwhelming, over-decorated Vanderbilt house to drive to Grand Central Station, Lydia knew that both the Earl and her father heaved a sigh of relief.

"It is like having a surfeit of *pâté de foie gras!*" Sir Robert remarked dryly.

"I agree with you," the Earl said, "but they are exceedingly kind and generous people, and we have been lent for our journey the Commodore's own private Rail-Road Car which is known as *The Duchess*."

"I am sure we will find the name is a very appropriate one!" Sir Robert remarked.

He was right in his assumption. The Rail-Road Car was far larger, more elaborate and ornate than the one owned by the Earl.

There were four bedrooms, a Drawing-Room with chairs that were so comfortable that sitting down felt like sinking into a cloud.

Everything was upholstered in the richest damask and the carpets on the floor were so thick that their feet seemed to sink down into them.

To Lydia it was as fascinating as being in an elaborate dolls'-house.

She explored the whole car, admired the kitchen, and even peeped into the rooms which the servants who travelled with them occupied, sleeping in bunk-beds arranged one above the other. The Earl's valet and her father's were in the next coach.

"It is quite fascinating!" she exclaimed.

Heloise sinking into a comfortable chair merely said:

"I hope it does not rock, or I shall feel as if I am still at sea!"

"Sit in the center and not above the wheels," Lydia said, "and you will see the magnificent countryside through which we will be passing. Think of it, Heloise! We shall actually see the Rocky Mountains!"

Heloise did not bother to answer, but merely looked apathetic until the Earl sat down beside her.

Then she flirted with him very prettily so that Lydia felt she could slip away into the background and sit at the window looking out, determined to miss nothing.

And yet all the time she was watching the scenery she could not help being conscious that the Earl was not far away from her.

When she was alone in her comfortable bed she found herself thinking about him and going over once again the conversation they had had aboard ship.

'Perhaps I shall have another chance to talk to him alone,' she thought.

She knew it was going to be difficult when Heloise was always there and angry if she asserted herself in any way or even talked when she should have remained silent.

It had been very cold in New York, and now there was thick snow outside the City which made the land through which they were passing look white and enchanting.

When she woke and had a glimpse of it through her bedroom window she got up early though it was, thinking she would be able to see better from the Drawing-Room.

She was in fact, so early that there was not even a sign of the servants. She drew up a blind and sat looking out.

The landscape stretching away into an indefinite distance was so lovely that she decided this would always be something to remember.

She had been there for nearly half-an-hour when a steward came in.

He seemed surprised to see her there before he said a hearty 'good-morning!' and started to tidy up the Drawing-Room and draw up the rest of the blinds.

Without her asking for it he brought her some coffee and put it in front of her.

She sat thinking how exciting everything was, until as the Earl joined her she knew this was what she had been waiting for.

"I somehow felt you would be unable to sleep and miss the view," he said.

"It is so beautiful!" Lydia replied. "Exactly what I thought America would be like."

The Earl raised his eyebrows and as if she had to explain she said:

"Very big, stimulating to the imagination, and asking for development which will spoil it!"

The Earl laughed.

"It is a new country with new ideas," he said, "and you are quite right. Every time I come here I feel my imagination stimulated by something new."

"I am so glad you feel like that."

"Why?"

"Because when I have seen you out hunting I somehow thought you were restricted by the smallness of the country, not only by the fields and hedges, but by the social world in which you live."

She paused. Then she said:

"I hope I am not being rude, but I did not realise that you were 'thinking big.'"

The Earl laughed again.

"I suppose I should be insulted, but instead I can only justify myself by saying that I am investing in quite a number of new projects in America, and I am hoping some of their progressive ideas will be taken up by the British."

"I have never read anything about this in your speeches in the House of Lords," Lydia remarked.

"You have read my speeches?"

Too late she thought that perhaps what she had said had been too revealing.

The colour rose in her cheeks as she answered a little evasively:

"I am always interested in reforms."

"Then you are certainly different from most women

whose only idea of reform is whether they should change their hair-style for a different one or not," the Earl replied cynically.

"I am sure that is unfair," Lydia said quickly. "Perhaps when you are talking to them they think they should just listen and not try to force their ideas and opinions on you."

The Earl's eyes twinkled.

"It is certainly unusual for a woman to be anxious to defend her own sex, but then, Miss Westbury, you are very unusual."

"Now I think you are being unkind," Lydia said. "You know as well as I do that I am a very ordinary person."

She nearly added: "In comparison with Heloise!" then thought that was obvious without her emphasising the fact.

As if once again he read her thoughts the Earl said quietly:

"That is the only unintelligent thing you have said since we first met!"

"It is true," Lydia insisted because she felt she had to.

"Then we must disagree."

As he spoke Sir Robert came into the Drawing-Room and sat down beside them.

"I have had an excellent night!" he exclaimed. "If there is one thing the Americans know how to make better than anybody else it is a comfortable bed!"

Lydia knew now that her father was there it would be impossible to go on talking to the Earl.

It had been a sheer delight when they had duelled in words and she had known that she stimulated his mind as he stimulated hers.

But now it was her duty to go to see if Heloise was awake.

She had finished her breakfast which the stewards had brought to them together with the morning newspapers which had been picked up at the first station at which they stopped.

She knew there would be many things for her to do for her sister and that for the rest of the morning she would be kept busy helping her to dress.

chapter four

OWING to the bad weather there were frequent delays on the journey by train which actually Lydia enjoyed.

Instead of stopping for only a short time at the wayside stations they would be held up for perhaps two or even three hours.

When this happened the Earl and Sir Robert said they must have some exercise, and they would walk off into the countryside having instructed the guard to signal them by bursts on the engine's whistle when it was time for them to return.

Whenever it was possible and Heloise would allow it, Lydia went with them.

She had been sensible enough knowing where they were going, to pack the thick boots she wore at home, and since it was so cold her father had bought her, at one of the stations, a fur coat made from white goat-skins.

He had given Heloise a sable coat at Christmas when Lydia's present had been just two books.

The goat-skin was the warmest coat she had ever owned and when she wore it she looked part of the snow scene as she tramped beside the two men, finding it hard at times to keep up with the pace set by the Earl.

It was wildly exciting not only because she had stepped into a world she had never known before, but also because she was with him.

As her father walked with them she did not join much in the conversation but listened, knowing that every day she was falling more and more in love.

While she admitted to herself that it was hopeless to love a man who belonged to her sister, she knew that the Earl had captured her heart and she would never love anybody else.

She found it difficult not to be angry with Heloise because she wasted so many opportunities of being with the man to whom she was engaged.

"Come with us, Heloise," Lydia pleaded. "You will feel much better in the fresh air, and it is so enchanting to see everything white with snow. The beauty of the mountains in the distance will make you feel as if you had stepped onto another Planet."

"I am quite content with this one," Heloise replied sharply, "and if you think I am going to trudge about in the snow ruining my skin with the wind, you are very much mistaken!"

She would therefore either lie in bed or else sit in the Drawing-Room, looking when they returned exquisitely lovely in one of her expensive and elaborate gowns.

The Earl and Sir Robert on their walks would have been talking animatedly on all sorts of different subjects—Politics, horses, international finance, or the ever-expanding British Empire.

Yet when they entered the Rail Road Car to find Heloise waiting for them, Lydia knew that the Earl suddenly fell silent and she thought it must be because he was overwhelmed by her beauty and words were superfluous.

She then hurried to her own room, forcing herself not to feel jealous because she had known from the very beginning that it was impossible for her to compete in any way with Heloise.

"I will just have to be thankful to God that I have met anybody so wonderful," she whispered to herself, "and have come on this exciting journey where I can be near him. How could I possibly be greedy enough to ask for more?"

Her body told her there was a great deal more she wanted, but her mind which she had disciplined for so many years made her think what she called 'sensibly.'

Because she felt guilty at being in love with her sister's *fiancé* she waited on Heloise, if it was possible, even more arduously and tried every morning to find a way of making her look even more lovely than she was already, by arranging her hair in different styles.

Not that she got any thanks for it.

Heloise, bored with the journey, took it out on Lydia because there was nobody else.

"I am sick of this train!" she said a thousand times when they were alone together. "I want to go to Balls. I cannot think why we did not stay in New York for the one which Mrs. Vanderbilt was giving, and I am sure when we do arrive at this dead-and-alive place on the other side of the world, it will be as boring as this is, if not more so!"

"How can you know that until you reach Honolulu?" Lydia asked. "And think how lovely it will be to see the sun and feel really warm!"

"I hope you remembered to pack all my sunshades," Heloise said. "You know how delicate my skin is and must not get sunburnt."

"Yes, of course I remembered and put in all the ones that match your gowns," Lydia replied, "and you also have some big shady hats."

When they reached the Rocky Mountains Lydia was so excited that she tried to imbue Heloise with some of her own delight at everything she saw.

It was not only the beauty of the mountains themselves, but the glaciers, the half-frozen rivers, and the incredible engineering feat which had been achieved in building a railroad through to California!

There were also the people they saw at every stop.

Here at last, Lydia had a sight of the strange and different types of people who she knew had come to California in the Gold Rush and whose descendants were still struggling to find gold.

Forty thousand immigrants had, she learned, arrived from Europe, South America and Mexico, and Australia sent its 'Sydney Ducks' who were frequently ex-convicts.

There were also the Chinese who helped to build

the railways and there seemed to be a mixed collection of nationalities at every station.

Lydia looked at them with wide eyes, but Heloise would not even go to the window of the Rail Road Car to look.

"Why should I concern myself with a lot of common, rough people like that?" she asked.

Lydia knew she was thinking of the aristocrats she had met in London and was resenting travelling further and further away from what she called 'civilisation,' even though the Earl was with her.

When they stopped at a station at the foot of one of the highest mountains and were told they could explore the tiny hamlet outside for an hour before the train moved off again, Lydia set out with the Earl and her father.

But they had only gone a little way before Sir Robert stopped and said he had a blister on his heel and intended to return to the train.

"Go on without me," he said. "It is nothing serious and I will tell my valet not to give me these boots again."

He walked away and Lydia looked a little apprehensively at the Earl.

"Do you mind if I come with you?" she asked.

"I should be very disappointed if I have to go alone," the Earl replied. "I want you to tell me your impressions of what you have seen so far."

"It is fascinating beyond words!"

"I saw you looking intently at the different types of people who were on the station just now," he said. "It was almost as if you were looking for something."

She smiled because she thought that was what he

was always doing, and replied:

"I was thinking that the Gold Rush symbolised something which all men—and women for that matter—want."

"Gold?" the Earl asked cynically.

"No, hope!" Lydia answered. "I am convinced that it was not only greed that brought so many people here in 1849 from every part of the world. It was hope which turned them into explorers, hope which sustained them through the incredible hardships they endured, which of course resulted in many of them dying."

"I have never heard it explained like that before," the Earl remarked.

"I think it is the same feeling that made the heroes of legend go out in search of the Golden Fleece and the Holy Grail, and it was hope that stimulated Captain Cook to go further and further on his voyage of discovery until of course he finally found Hawaii."

"And what do you hope to find?" the Earl enquired.

As if she was surprised at his suddenly becoming personal Lydia thought before she replied:

"I have always hoped for many things which I never imagined for one moment would ever really materialise, and yet, incredibly and unbelievably, through you I have been able to find my 'crock of gold at the end of the rainbow.'"

"And you think that will suffice you for the rest of your life?"

Lydia laughed.

"I think it will probably have to do so. But when I go home I shall keep praying and hoping there will be a chance for me to see other parts of the world and discover treasures which before I could only read about in my books."

They walked on in silence, the only sound being the crispness of the hard crisp snow breaking under their feet.

Then there was the hoot of the engine in the distance and the Earl turned round.

"We must go back."

Lydia looked ahead at the untouched whiteness of the ground and gave a deep sigh.

"I wonder how many explorers have felt frustrated when, having got so far, they have had to turn back."

She was speaking more to herself than to the Earl, but he replied:

"There is always tomorrow."

"That is what we all hope," Lydia said. "At the same time one always feels if one could just go a little further, just reach the next horizon to see if it is within our grasp."

There was silence for a moment, then the Earl said:

"Supposing when you find it there are reasons why you cannot make it yours?"

"Then of course," Lydia answered, "you can only go on hoping that perhaps by a miracle, by fighting, will-power, or prayer you will be successful."

She was thinking as she spoke that the Earl would be successful in anything he wanted, and because of the force of his personality he was inevitably the victor, the conqueror, and it would be impossible for anybody to gainsay him.

Then as she looked at him, wondering what he would reply, she saw he was looking serious and she had the feeling their conversation had changed from being just light-hearted and stimulating.

Then as they walked on he said:

"You have given me a great deal to think about, although there are some things to which there appears to be no solution."

"I do not believe that," Lydia said. "Not for you, at any rate. And if we fail because we are small and ineffectual, I believe there is always a Power to help us if we call upon it."

As she spoke she thought perhaps it was a very strange thing to say to the Earl of Royston, and might almost sound as if she was preaching at him.

It seemed to her as if it was a long time before he answered:

"I hope you are right, Lydia."

It was the first time he had called her by her Christian name, and she felt her heart turn a somersault because she had never known it to sound so attractive until she heard him say it.

Only yesterday when they had taken a short walk from another station he had called her 'Miss Westbury,' and her father had said:

"For goodness sake, Royston, call her Lydia! After all, she is going to be your sister-in-law. When you say 'Miss Westbury' it reminds me of one of my sisters who was an ugly and tiresome woman, who never found a man who was fool enough to marry her!"

The Earl had laughed, but he had not called her 'Lydia' until now.

Because it made her so happy she was smiling and her face must have been radiant as they climbed back into the train.

She went at once to Heloise to see if there was

anything she could do for her.

Her sister looked at her and said disagreeably:

"What have you got to smile about, I would like to know? And you had no right to stay with Hunter after Papa came back with a bad foot! You should have returned too!"

The way she spoke and the expression in her eyes wiped the smile from Lydia's lips.

"I am sorry, Heloise," she said, "I did not think of it, and I was enjoying the exercise."

"Well, in future," Heloise ordered, "you will keep away from Hunter, if I am not with him. I want him to be alone and miss me, and I am sure your stupid chatter only irritates him."

Lydia said nothing. She merely went to take off her fur coat and her thick boots.

As she did so she wondered humbly if, in fact, the Earl found their talks together boring and stupid.

Then she told herself that although it might seem conceited she was certain he was as stimulated by the subjects they discussed as she was.

Although with her father he talked of ordinary matters the moment they were alone it seemed as if he was as eager as she was to discuss more fundamental subjects, which she knew Heloise would not understand.

"He is so different from what I expected," she told herself.

As the train began to move out of the station Lydia began counting the days when she would still be on the train with the Earl, and however disagreeable her sister might be, she knew she could not be prevented from talking to him, if she had the chance.

Once they were through the Rocky Mountains and in California, it was only a short journey before they arrived in San Francisco.

Lydia had been hoping that they would see something of the City which she felt would be fascinating, and which her books had told her had grown up from a dusty, remote village called *Yerba Buena* which meant 'the place of the good herb.'

The story of how it had begun with the Missions which came from Spain, then grown with the Russian-American Fur Company, and finally with the American occupation, was fascinating.

California had been a land of unrest and conspiracy with a wide-spread mistrust of foreigners until the Gold Rush turned it into a modern Babel.

Lydia would not have known so much about San Francisco if, at one of the larger stations at which they stopped she had not given a cry of delight when she saw there were books for sale on a stall.

"Books!" she had exclaimed. "Oh, please, Papa, let me buy some!"

The Earl heard what she said and exclaimed:

"Now I know what is missing in *The Duchess!* I had a feeling that the famous Commodore had forgotten something of importance, but I could not think what it could be."

"I suppose he was so busy poring over his plans that he had not the time to think of anything else," Lydia said with a smile.

"But of course when we were in New York, I should have thought we would need books."

"Please," Lydia said quickly, "I am not complaining!"

"Of course not, but I promise you when we return I will see there is a stack of books of every description to keep you interested."

He then proceeded to buy every book, although there were not many, that was available, and did the same at every other station where there was any literature for sale apart from the local newspapers.

Lydia therefore found herself with a very miscellaneous collection.

There were cheap novelettes some of which she fancied had been collected from the train after their owners had left them behind, religious tracts and true adventure stories.

She, however, was most grateful for the primitive but very interesting guide-books that had been written about various parts of America.

Because San Francisco was now so important a city Lydia was disappointed when she heard the Earl say:

"The battleship which is to carry us to Hawaii will, I am certain, have been waiting impatiently for our arrival, and we must therefore go straight on board from the station."

Lydia did not express her disappointment, but Heloise said:

"If the sea is rough I cannot bear it!"

"I think that is very unlikely," the Earl smiled. "We will now be on the Pacific Ocean and it will be growing warmer every day until you will find it very hot by the time we reach Hawaii."

"I hope you have packed all the right clothes, Lydia," Heloise said when they were alone. "I shall be extremely angry if I am not the smartest and most outstanding person at the Coronation!"

"Excepting the Queen," Lydia smiled. "You can hardly want to overshadow the leading lady of the day."

"Why not?" Heloise asked.

"Because it would be unkind," Lydia explained. "Actually she will be very resplendent because the King ordered two crowns when he was in Europe from an English Jewellers."

"Crowns or no crowns," Heloise said, "I want everybody to look at me! The moment we arrive in Honolulu you must press all my gowns, and make quite certain that my hats have not been crushed by all this tedious travelling."

"Do not worry," Lydia said. "You will look lovely! I am sure everybody will be overwhelmed by you."

She thought as Heloise was ready to leave the train that nobody could have looked lovelier.

Because it was quite warm in San Francisco she was wearing a silk gown in her favourite shade of blue with a small velvet coatee over it and an elegant hat trimmed with flowers of the same colour which seemed to accentuate the gold of her hair and the translucence of her skin.

There were officers of the ship's company to meet them on the station, and Lydia quickly realised that from now on the Earl was being treated as the Queen's Representative and would be accorded every possible honour by the British.

They drove in an open carriage down to the dock and she had her first glimpse of San Francisco's fantastic roads which went straight up and down the hills on which the town was built so that the horses had great difficulty in not slipping, and on some slopes had to zig-zag to reach the top.

All too soon they reached the harbour and amongst the hundreds of ships which made up the fishing fleet with their high masts and their white sails was waiting for them, the British Battleship, *HMS Victorious*.

It was, although Lydia was not aware of it, a very old ship which had been sent to the Pacific for the last years of her life before she was taken to the scrap-yard.

However she looked extremely smart with her crew all wearing white covers on their caps, and their white summer uniforms with bell-bottom trousers.

The Earl and his party were piped aboard and were welcomed by the Captain who was wearing a large number of medals.

He made a brief speech of welcome to the Earl who replied and then they were taken below to their cabins.

These were very different from those they had enjoyed on the *Etruria*.

The Earl was given the Captain's cabin, which was the largest and had a Sitting-Room attached to it, while the rest of the party were accommodated in the cabins of the officers.

These Lydia learnt, had been moved down in order of seniority, and she was sorry for the midshipmen who had obviously been pushed out into any hole or corner they could find to accommodate them.

Her cabin was exactly the same as Heloise's, small but well fitted and quite comfortable.

Heloise complained volubly.

"It is far too tiny," she said scornfully. "I shall feel as if I am in my coffin!"

"Oh, Heloise, do not say such things!" Lydia begged. "It is unlucky!"

"At least there are Englishmen aboard," Heloise went on, "and I have every intention of looking pretty tonight, so start unpacking my things!"

It was impossible for Heloise's enormous amount of luggage to fit into her cabin, so some of her trunks had to be left outside in the passage.

Lydia had to find the one which contained the gown she wished to wear and all the accessories that went with it.

It took her so long to get Heloise ready in time for dinner that she only had a few minutes to change her own clothes. She realised as she did so, that the ship had already put to sea.

There was, she thought, hardly any swell as they left harbour and moved a little way along the coast before setting out into the Pacific Ocean.

At dinner when she was sitting next to a young and enthusiastic officer who was obviously delighted to talk to her he told her that it would take five days to reach Honolulu.

"We are all looking forward to the Coronation," he said, "and if it is anything like the usual Hawaiian Festivities it will go on for days!"

He sounded so delighted at what lay ahead that Lydia was certain he was visualising how pretty the dancers would be and that he would make the very most of his time ashore.

She had learned from one of her books how much

Hawaiians liked the English, and that in the early days the women had welcomed men from overseas offering themselves with a generosity that was unsurpassed by any other nationality.

As she expected, every officer on the ship was overwhelmed by Heloise.

They stared at her as if they did not believe she was real, and their admiration made her blossom like a rose turning its face to the sun.

She became animated and flirted charmingly with every man who spoke to her, and her laughter was spontaneous and very attractive.

Almost as if she had been touched by a magic wand, Lydia thought, she had changed from the petulant, bored young woman who had sulked on the train, unless she was with the Earl.

Even then she had continually complained about the rumble of the wheels and her feeling that she was being confined in what she described as a 'cattle truck.'

'I wish she was always like this,' Lydia thought wistfully.

Because she assumed that the Earl was as entranced as everybody else, she did not look at him.

Instead she set out to make the elderly officer who sat on her other side tell her of the voyages he had made in *HMS Victorious* in other parts of the Pacific.

He did not make his experiences sound very interesting, and she had to force herself not to keep thinking of the Earl, or trying to listen to what he was saying.

The next day, to her surprise, Heloise rose quite early and went up on deck.

There were plenty of officers to find her a comfortable place to sit out of the sun and to talk and flirt with her whenever they got the opportunity.

The Earl on the other hand spent quite a lot of time on the bridge with the Captain, and Lydia knew that he was extremely interested in all aspects of the ship and was therefore escorted all over it.

Only once did she have the chance the next day to speak to him alone.

It was after luncheon and Heloise had been helped by one of the officers with whom they had eaten into a deck-chair making quite certain it was sheltered from the sun and the wind, and as far as possible from any movement of the sea.

She was looking particularly alluring in a white gown trimmed with green ribbons, her sunshade was green, and camelias with their dark green leaves decorated the wide brim of her hat.

She looked as if she had just stepped out of the Royal Enclosure at Ascot, and it was understandable that every man on the ship was ready to lay his heart at her feet.

Because she was not needed Lydia moved away to stand in the stern watching the churning water from their wake dwindle away into the distance.

She thought she could see a porpoise—or was it a sea-lion—and was straining her eyes to decide which it was when a voice beside her said:

"It is a dolphin. You will see a lot of them when we reach Hawaii, and they are very playful."

She gave a little start and turned her face towards the Earl.

"I was expecting porpoises, sea-lions, or perhaps a whale."

"Given the chance you will see them all!"

"I do hope so!"

She spoke with such enthusiasm that the Earl said:

"Are you intending to study the flora and fauna of Hawaii, as well as everything else?"

"Of course," Lydia replied, "and most of all, I want to see the 'Hawaiian Honeycreepers.'"

He gave a short laugh.

"Again you have surprised me, Lydia. I have never yet met a woman who travelled to some strange country who was more interested in its Honeycreepers than its King!"

"I mean no disrespect to His Majesty," Lydia answered, "but that is the truth, and I cannot help feeling that, however resplendently everybody may dress themselves for the Coronation, they will not equal the flowers we shall see in Hawaii, unless of course the books you bought for me on the subject were lying!"

She gave a little laugh and before he could speak she added;

"And do not dare tell me I shall be disappointed. I am determined not to be!"

"I would not dream of doing anything of the sort," he said. "That would deprive you of your 'hope.' I know that is more important to you than anything else."

She was surprised that he had remembered their conversation, and said:

"I have a feeling—and because of my Celtic blood my feelings are often right—that Hawaii will not only live up to my expectations and hopes, but exceed them!"

"That is exactly what I hope too," the Earl said.

Without saying any more he walked away and left her, and she stared after him a little puzzled.

There had been a serious note in his voice that was inescapable, and she wondered what he was hoping for and why it was so important to him.

'He has everything,' she thought to herself, 'and Heloise!'

She knew if she thought of the Earl and Heloise together there was a sharp little pain within her breast which she tried to ignore, but which seemed to grow, day by day.

"No couple could be more suited to each other," she kept telling herself. "He is so handsome and she so beautiful!"

Then some critical voice at the back of her mind asked her if beauty alone would ever be enough for somebody like the Earl.

"Of course it will," she insisted, "and Heloise will grace the Royston diamonds as no other woman could possibly do. When he sees her at the head of the table he will know that she is exactly the right wife, who those who admire him would have chosen for him."

She was thinking of the Earl when she was joined by the young officer who had sat next to her at dinner the first night they arrived.

"I want to talk to you, Miss Westbury," he said.

"What about?" Lydia enquired.

"What do you think? About you of course!" he replied. "I suppose you know that to have you with us in the ship is like being given a glass of water in a dry and very thirsty desert!"

Lydia laughed.

"Very poetic!" she said, "but you can hardly expect me to believe anything like that when I have been reading about the beauty of the girls in Hawaii, and I am certain that Honolulu and any other place at which you call abounds with beautiful women!"

"But they are not English," he said, "and while they are exotic, to me there is nothing more lovely and exciting than an English girl like yourself!"

"You flatter me!" Lydia laughed.

She could not take him seriously, but he tried to go on flirting with her.

At the same time it made her feel not so insignificant as she did when she was at home.

When she sat next to the same young man at dinner that night he continued to pay her compliments and, although she told herself she was being very stupid, in a way they warmed her heart.

All too quickly for Lydia four days had passed and the Captain told her that tomorrow they would see the volcanic mountain of Hawaii.

"If it is erupting," he said, "it will be a bad omen for the King, which will not go unnoticed by his subjects."

"Does it often do that?" Lydia enquired.

"Fairly often," he replied. "Sometimes it just has smoke coming out of the crater. At others there is a certain amount of burning lava rolling down the side of it. But no one takes much notice, and it is not very serious."

On the last evening of their voyage, the Captain arranged for a Band to play after dinner.

At first, while they sat out in the moonlight, the Band played more or less classical music.

Then, and perhaps it was Heloise who suggested it, they broke into dance tunes and both Heloise and Lydia were claimed at once by two eager young officers.

It was something Lydia had not expected, but which she enjoyed, quite content to play second fiddle to Heloise.

She soon found that the English had adopted the American fashion of 'cutting in' during a dance so that she was passed from one man to another.

She found also to her surprise, that most of them were exceedingly good dancers.

She was sure that as far as Heloise was concerned the evening could go on forever, but the Captain ended the gaieties at midnight.

The Band played 'God Save the Queen' and they all stood to attention, after which they went to bed.

"I have enjoyed myself!" Heloise said, as Lydia helped her out of her gown. "If it could always be like tonight I would not mind the voyage going on for longer!"

"It has been as calm as a mill-pond," Lydia answered.

Even as she spoke she felt the ship give a lurch and was aware that the wind was beginning to whistle through the shrouds.

She hoped Heloise had not noticed it, and because she was busy reciting all the many compliments she had received during the evening she got into bed without complaining.

By the time Lydia had reached her own cabin the

ship was beginning to pitch and toss.

She thought with dismay that Heloise would be ill again and she would have to attend to her instead of, as she had hoped, being able to see the ship coming into port at Honolulu.

The wind was certainly getting up and by the time she was in bed the whole structure seemed to be creaking almost deafeningly, and her shoes, which she had not put away in the cupboard, were sliding backwards and forwards on the floor of her cabin.

She listened but could not hear Heloise calling for her and was sure therefore that she had not yet been disturbed.

'It has been lovely weather up until now,' she thought.

But she knew from her books that sudden squalls and very strong winds could get up at a moment's notice around the Hawaiian Islands, and the weather could change, as one said—'in the twinkling of an eye.'

"I am sure it will be calm again by tomorrow," Lydia told herself consolingly.

Instead the wind seemed to be increasing and growing really violent.

She was however not frightened, thinking it impossible to feel anything but secure in a British Battleship.

Then quite suddenly there was a ringing of bells in a way that seemed almost deafening, and the sound of raised voices.

The next minute the door to her cabin burst open and a voice said:

"Fire! Get up on deck immediately!"

Lydia gave a cry of horror and jumped out of bed.

She groped her way in the darkness to the door and moved into Heloise's cabin.

Her sister was sitting up in bed having been awakened in the same way, and she was screaming.

"What is happening? What is happening? Where is the fire?"

"It is all right, dearest," Lydia said calmly. "But we have to go up on deck as we have been told to do."

"I am . . . frightened!"

"I know, but you will be quite safe! You may have to get into a small boat, but I am sure we are not far from land."

"I shall drown—I know I shall!" Heloise wailed.

Even as she spoke the Earl's authoritative voice said from the doorway:

"Hurry! I am waiting to take you up on deck. Put on a warm coat, but do not worry about anything else."

Then Lydia heard her father say:

"I will go ahead to see that the boat is ready for the two girls."

The way he spoke told Lydia all too clearly, that things were very serious.

chapter five

THE Earl had a lantern with him, and while he lighted
the cabin with it, Lydia opened the door of the wardrobe and groped amongst the clothes in it for Heloise's
sable coat.

By the time she had with difficulty found it, Heloise
was screaming.

"I am not—going in a—small boat!" she cried.
"I shall—drown in the—sea! I want to—stay here."

The Earl did not speak and Lydia forced her sister's
arms into the arms of the coat as she said quietly:

"You will be quite safe, Heloise, everybody will
look after you."

"I will not go—I will—not!" Heloise screamed
and now her voice was completely hysterical.

Lydia looked towards the Earl.

"I think you will have to carry her."

Still without saying anything he handed her the lantern and picked Heloise up in his arms.

For a moment she tried to struggle against him, then half-sobbing, half-screaming, she put her face against his shoulder.

He carried her out into the passage and walking behind them Lydia lighted the way.

As she passed her cabin door she realised she was wearing only the nightgown in which she had slept.

As if the Earl was aware of it at the same time he said:

"Put on a thick coat and follow as quickly as you can."

For a moment Lydia hesitated, thinking that it might be difficult for him to reach the companion-way in the dark.

Then she saw lights at the top of it and knew that other people on the ship were carrying lanterns.

The ship gave a lurch as she entered her cabin and almost threw her to the floor, but she managed to prop the lantern up on the dressing-table before she reached for the wardrobe.

Now the ship was rolling so badly that she thought it would be a mistake to linger, and instead of finding her coat she merely took a blanket off the bed and threw it over her shoulders.

She picked up the lantern again and went back into the passage.

She could see ahead that the Earl with Heloise in his arms had just reached the top of the companion-way.

She was about to follow him when she heard a voice calling:

"Help! Help!"

She paused on the bottom step wondering if she should go on, then again there was a faint cry for help.

Holding the lantern high to illuminate as much ground as possible she moved a little way down the passage and saw there was somebody lying on the ground.

"Please—help me!" a young voice cried.

Now by the light of the lantern swinging in her hand she saw it was one of the midshipmen.

"Are you hurt?" she asked.

"I think I have—broken my—leg."

He spoke bravely but she could see there were tears of pain in his eyes.

"I was running to warn His Lordship of the fire in the Engine Room, as I had been ordered to do," he said, "but I—slipped."

"Perhaps it is only a bad sprain," Lydia said, "but you will have to be carried up on deck. I will find somebody."

She turned to go towards the companion-way, but as she did so the boy asked:

"You will not forget about me?"

He sounded like a frightened child, and she replied:

"I promise I would not do that."

For a moment the ship seemed a little more steady although she was sure the wind was whipping the waves up into a tempest.

Then as she reached the bottom step she saw the Earl coming down obviously in search of her.

"Come along!" he said. "I was worried about why you were taking so long."

He reached her as he spoke and she replied:

"One of the midshipmen has broken his leg. He cannot walk, and if he is left here he may be forgotten."

She looked at the Earl pleadingly as she spoke and thought he hesitated for a moment before he said:

"Your father and Heloise are already in the boat and they are waiting for you."

"Please come to carry the boy," she said quickly. "He is in great pain and unable to move."

The Earl did not argue, and as she was already hurrying back towards the midshipman, he followed her.

"Here is somebody to help you," Lydia said cheerfully.

The Earl bent down and picked the boy up in his arms.

"I am going to carry you in a 'Fireman's lift,'" he said, "because it is easier."

He put him over his shoulder, his head down his back.

Then because the ship was rolling again the Earl steadied himself with his hand on the wall before he reached the railing of the companion-way.

He went up it quickly and Lydia following thought how strong he was, but she found it difficult and wished she had taken a little longer to find her coat.

As it was, the blanket trailed onto the ground, and she found it impossible to lift it out of the way and at the same time hold onto the railing and the lantern.

When she reached the top of the stairway she found

that the Earl had already disappeared on the deck with the boy over his shoulder and there were lanterns hanging from hooks on the walls.

There was therefore no need for her to carry hers any further and as she handed it to the first sailor she saw, he said:

"Hurry up, Miss! Get into one of the boats as quickly as you can!"

Lydia walked unsteadily towards the door that led out onto the deck and the moment she stepped out she felt as if the wind swept her off her feet.

For a moment it was impossible to see anything except the waves that were illuminated by the moonlight, and seemed as they broke over the side of the ship determined to sink her.

The decks were awash, but now Lydia realised there was a light coming from the ship itself and that it was the light of the flames that had started in the Engine Room.

As she looked at it holding onto the doorway she saw the Earl coming towards her and realised the boat into which he had put the midshipman was already being lowered down the side of the ship into the sea.

He reached her and said sharply:

"Why did you take so long? You should have gone in that boat!"

"I am sorry," Lydia said humbly.

"There is another one," he said, "and this time I do not intend you to be left behind."

As he spoke he took her arm and led her along the deck to where the sailors were lowering another lifeboat.

The officer saw them and turned to say:

"Please hurry, M'Lord. We're having difficulty in this sea."

He spoke quite calmly and the Earl replied:

"We are doing our best, Officer."

As he spoke a wave splashed over the rails and covered both him and Lydia with spray.

She felt the salt water running down her face, and as it was also in her eyes it was hard to see.

The Earl dragged her forward and a moment later she was lifted up and placed in the boat.

She wanted to put out her hands to hold onto him and beg him to come too.

Then to her relief she heard the officer say:

"Get in, M'Lord. We cannot take to the boats ourselves until all our passengers are accounted for."

The Earl climbed in sitting down beside Lydia and, as if it were the most natural thing to do, he put his arm around her and held her close to him.

Then in what seemed to her only a very few seconds the boat was full and lowered into the sea.

As they reached the water they were soaked by the spray and the boat itself was plunging up and down in what Lydia thought was a terrifying manner.

Yet because she was beside the Earl and his arm was holding her, she was not really frightened. She knew however, that by this time Heloise would be frantic and was doubtless still screaming.

The sailors pulled away from the ship, rowing strongly, but at the same time finding it extremely difficult to hold the boat in any degree of steadiness in such a violent sea.

More and more waves splashed over them, and as Lydia saw one of the seamen start bailing out the water which was rising round their feet the Earl asked:

"Can you swim?"

"Yes," Lydia replied, "but I have never swum in a sea as rough as this."

"Let us hope it will not be necessary," he said in a low voice, "but if we do have to take to the water hold onto me, and I will look after you."

It was what she wanted to hear, and it flashed through her mind that if they were drowned together she would not mind because she would not be alone.

At the same time she wanted to live, and she was sure that the Earl would survive because, as she had thought before, he was always the victor, the conqueror, a man who always won through whatever the odds against him.

It was impossible to see at all far, for although there was a moon overhead the light from it was intermittent.

At the same time the wind was so strong that Lydia felt as if as it beat against her face it blew her hair high into the air, and distorted everything.

The Earl looked back and Lydia also turning her head could now see the ship heaving up and down, the centre of it brilliant with the light from the fire, the flames leaping up against the darkness.

"How could this have happened?" she asked in a low voice.

The wind almost swept the words from her lips, but the Earl heard them.

"She is an old ship," he said. "It will be difficult to save her."

The boat they were in was swamped again by a huge wave.

Then as the officer gave sharp orders one after another, a wave that seemed to loom up above them like an avenging angel crashed down into the little boat so that the men rowing could do nothing but duck their heads as it fell on them.

In that moment the boat went out of control and almost before Lydia could realise what was happening she found herself tipped into the sea and its coldness engulfed her.

She came up gasping and felt the Earl's hand reach out towards her.

"Hold onto me!" he said sharply. "The shore is not far ahead."

She clutched at his coat and started to swim, striking out with her legs.

Her blanket had floated away and she felt relieved that she was wearing nothing but her nightgown which made it easier for her to swim.

Then there was another wave and she felt as if she was going down into the very depths of the ocean.

She came up again and thought she must be in the surf that beat against the beaches of Hawaii.

Before she even had time to breathe, another wave struck her so hard that it carried her a long way forward and she felt something strike her forehead.

Then there was nothing but darkness . . .

Lydia came back to consciousness slowly, and it took a little while before she was aware that she was lying on her back and there was sunshine.

For a moment she could not understand what had happened. Then she remembered.

Slowly she put her hand up to her forehead and found a place near her hair which hurt when she touched it.

Then as her memory told her that the ship had been on fire and the boat in which they had left it had overturned, she opened her eyes.

Above her she saw the waving green leaves of a palm-tree and knew she was lying on the sand.

She put her hand down as if to reassure herself it was not the water, then very slowly and with difficulty she sat up.

For a moment she thought she must be dreaming.

After the agony of the night, the roughness of the sea and the violence of the waves, she could hardly believe that just in front of her, now placidly lapping the shore, was the sea.

It was smooth and golden from the sun, with only a faint hint of foam as it moved gently in and out with a musical sound.

"It cannot be true!" Lydia told herself.

Then some distance out to sea she could see the grey outline of *HMS Victorious*.

The ship was still afloat, the fire was no longer burning, and she thought, although she could not be sure, that there was movement on the deck.

Now she looked about her and saw she was on the shore of a small sandy bay.

She had been lying in the shelter of some palm-trees, and behind her was the wild vegetation of the jungle.

It was certainly very beautiful with hibiscus flowering everywhere, as well as blossoms of yellow, pink, blue, cerise, orange and red, and dozens of other shades which she knew from her books must be the fragrant plumerias.

They were so lovely that she could only sit looking at them, finding it was hard to believe that they really existed apart from her imagination.

There were poinsettias and jacara, and a dozen other species she thought she recognised. Then suddenly as she stared in amazement, feeling because her head hurt her, bewildered and disorientated, she was aware that she was alone.

She had been so relieved in the first moments of regaining consciousness that she had only thought of how she had reached here and not who had been with her.

Now with a stab of her heart, she looked around, hoping that if she was here the Earl would be here too, and perhaps he was lying somewhere near on the sand.

But there was no one and the only sound was of the birds singing in the trees and bushes.

"Where can he be?" Lydia asked herself.

Then with a knife-pain that seemed to strike through her she was suddenly afraid.

It had not before struck her that though she was alive, he might be drowned.

Now she struggled to her feet, feeling that she must go and look for him and wondering frantically where he could be.

Then an agony of fear ran through her veins like a poison and made her think that perhaps after she had struck something which had rendered her unconscious he had saved her life and in doing so, lost his own.

"Oh, God, do not let that have happened!" she prayed. "He must be . . . safe, he must . . . be!"

She looked around wildly, staring out to sea as if she felt she might see his body floating in it.

Then she tried to search in the thickness of the vegetation, but knew she could not force her way through the bushes, to look for him.

Then commonsense told her that he would not be likely to be hiding from her in the jungle, and if he was not in this bay, perhaps the sea had carried him further along the coast.

"I must find him! I must!"

She pushed back her hair from her forehead and realised that it was quite dry which told her she must have been on the beach for a long time.

Anyway, it was now early in the morning, and the sun was coming up the sky.

Although she had no means of knowing whether or not she was right, she guessed it was perhaps five o'clock or a little earlier.

Her legs felt weak and she knew that her whole body ached from the effort of swimming in a rough sea and being buffeted about as if she was nothing more than a piece of driftwood.

She knew she had to search for the Earl and the only decision she had to make was in which direction she should start looking.

As she took her first steps over the sand she saw coming round the trees at the very edge of the bay the tall figure of a man.

For a moment because she found it difficult to focus her eyes she had no idea who it could be.

She only saw that he was naked to the waist and it flashed through her mind that he might be an Hawaiian, and perhaps he was hostile as the Hawaiian Warriers had been to Captain Cook.

Then with a little cry of joy she saw that it was the Earl.

Without thinking, without considering, she ran towards him, speeding over the sand, forgetting everything but the wonder of knowing that he was safe.

She reached him with her arms outstretched and flung herself against him crying incoherently:

"You are...alive! Oh, thank God...you are ...alive!"

He caught her in his arms, then as she looked up at him her eyes and her whole face radiant because she had found him, his lips came down on hers.

It was no shock.

It was as if it was inevitable, ordained from the beginning of time, that after the horror through which she had passed he should come to her unharmed when she thought she had lost him.

She felt his lips hold her captive, and because it was everything she had longed for and thought she would never know, she surrendered herself to a rapture that enveloped her like a burning light.

She felt a streak of ecstasy seep through her so poignant, so sharp, that it was almost a pain as well as a rapture.

He kissed her until she felt as if she merged into him and was no longer herself.

114

He raised his head to look down at her for a moment. Then he was kissing her again, kissing her with long, slow demanding kisses which made her thrill with sensations she had never known existed.

She only knew she had reached Paradise and that nothing else existed but the Earl's arms, his lips and him.

Only when Lydia felt that nobody could know such glory and not die with the wonder of it did she give a little murmur and hide her face against his shoulder.

"I thought you were . . . dead!" she murmured. "I . . . I thought I had . . . lost you!"

"I am alive, my precious," the Earl said, "and so are you!"

He put his hand under her chin and turned her face up to his.

He kissed her gently in a way that was different from the possessive demands of his lips before.

"I was so . . . afraid," Lydia whispered.

His arms tightened around her and he said:

"Come and sit down, my darling. We shall be rescued later, but now I want to make sure that you are not hurt in any way."

"I am . . . all right."

She could hardly speak.

All she knew was that her love enveloped them both with a radiance that made it impossible to think of anything else except that she was close to the man she had loved for so long, and he had kissed her.

As if he knew what she was feeling he said quietly:

"How could I help it, when it is what I have wanted to do for so long?"

"You . . . wanted to . . . kiss me?"

"Of course I wanted to kiss you!" he said fiercely.

"But . . ."

"I know, I know," he interrupted, "there are so many 'buts,' so many things to come between us."

"But . . ." Lydia murmured again.

The Earl drew her to the foot of a plumeria tree, and they sat beneath it with its blossoms, in this case of pale pink, dropping down on them like blessings from above.

He put his arms around Lydia and as she moved closer to him she became aware that he was nearly naked.

He had nothing on except his trousers and she supposed he must have found his coat cumbersome when swimming and had shrugged it off when they were fighting against the overwhelming waves that had eventually carried them to the shore.

Instinctively she put her hands over her breasts and the Earl smiled before he said:

"There is no point, my darling, in trying to be modest at this particular moment. I want to thank God that we are alive and although you have a bruise on your forehead, I do not think it is very serious."

"I . . . I was unconscious!"

"Just as we reached the shore you hit your head against a piece of flotsam. I dragged you out of the water and knew it was only a temporary unconsciousness. Then after all you had been through you must have fallen asleep."

Lydia gave a little laugh.

"How could I have done anything so absurd?"

"It often happens," the Earl replied, "and after I

satisfied myself that you were safe I went to investigate where we were and how many others had been cast up also on this particular island."

"We are not alone?"

"Only in this bay," he replied. "The boat crew are further along the coast and since when I saw them they were very inadequately clothed, it would be best for you to stay here."

"I want to be with...you."

"And I want you to be with me, my precious," he said. "But God knows what we are going to do about each other."

Lydia had forgotten her sister and that the Earl was engaged to her, forgotten everything except that they were alone, that he had his arms around her and had kissed her.

Now she was suddenly overwhelmed by the way in which she had behaved.

She looked down her eye-lashes dark against her cheeks as she said:

"I...I am sorry...I suppose I should be ashamed."

"Nobody could be more wonderful," the Earl said quietly, "for you must know, my darling one, I love you."

She looked up at him in astonishment.

"Did you...really say that?"

"I will say it again, a thousand times if you like, but we are both aware that the real question is—what can we do about it?"

For a moment it did not seem to matter and Lydia asked:

"When did you know you...loved me?"

The Earl smiled and said:

"I think it was the first time we met. I saw your eyes, and because they were worried I found it impossible to think of anything else. I think also we were both aware that we vibrated to each other in a way that was unusual and which actually had never happened to me before."

She looked at him as if she found it hard to believe what he said.

Then he gave a short laugh.

"I know it sounds ridiculous and of course I have often been attracted at first sight, or amused, or infatuated by a woman's beauty, but never, and this is the truth, Lydia, never has it been the same as when I first saw you."

She gave a deep sigh.

"I think," she said in a very small voice, "that it is what I felt for you when I first saw you out hunting and thought that nobody could be more attractive or more fascinating."

"You are flattering me!"

She shook her head.

"It is not flattery. I am telling you what I felt, and I thought too that you looked like a buccaneer or a pirate, and as if you always got what you wanted, whatever it might be."

"I hope that is true," the Earl said in a serious voice, "for what I want, more than I have ever wanted anything in the whole world, is you!"

She looked at him as if she could hardly believe what he had said and he went on:

"Oh, my precious, you are so different from any other woman! I adore your unselfishness, the way you think of everybody else and never about yourself. I love your courage, and of course, the way you stimulate my mind."

Lydia gave a little laugh.

"As you stimulate mine."

"We were meant for each other," the Earl said, "and it is only through my own stupidity that we are in the position in which we find ourselves now."

Almost as if she had suddenly appeared beside them Lydia knew that Heloise was there, pushing them apart from each other, spoiling the rapture that she could feel vibrating between them, which joined them indivisibly as one person.

As if he felt that he must tell her about it, the Earl said:

"I have no excuse for making such a mess of things. It was just a stupid gesture of pride, for which I have lain awake night after night, cursing myself."

Because the pain in his voice showed her how much he was hurt by what he was saying, Lydia moved a little closer to him.

"I want you to know the truth," the Earl said, "and then, my darling, you must help me, because for the moment I have no idea how to help myself."

"Tell me about it."

"I became involved with a beautiful lady," the Earl explained, "and as you thought, she looked somewhat like your sister with fair hair, blue eyes and a clear, unblemished skin."

Because Lydia knew he was speaking of the Duchess of Dorchester, she did not interrupt and he went on:

"I was warned that her husband was jealous, and

that I could expect him to challenge me to a duel. That, as you know, is illegal but it does frequently happen. At least he would prevent me from seeing his wife again."

The Earl paused and Lydia asked in a voice so soft he could hardly hear it:

"What happened . . . then?"

She could hardly bear to hear what he was telling her, but at the same time she wanted to know the truth.

"The Duke was too clever to do either of those things," the Earl went on, "and instead he went to the Queen."

"The Queen!"

"He intimated to Her Majesty that a scandal would be detrimental both to his position at Court, and to mine."

Lydia drew in her breath.

"So the Queen sent you away!"

"Exactly!" the Earl replied. "She commanded me to represent her at the Coronation in Hawaii."

"And you had to obey her command."

"Of course. But I was afraid that people might suspect the reason for my departure and laugh, so to save my pride, I asked your sister to marry me."

"So that is how it was!" Lydia whispered.

"I had met her once or twice," the Earl continued, "and thought her very beautiful—in fact without exception, the most beautiful girl I had ever seen. For years my relatives have been begging me to marry and I thought my engagement would be a snub to those who would be only too quick to say that I had been rebuked by Her Majesty for behaving like a naughty boy!"

"I . . . understand," Lydia said softly.

"My darling, I knew you would," he said. "But how could I have known, how could I have guessed that in doing so I would crucify myself?"

He paused before he said:

"I have never, and this is the truth, never been in love, until I met you."

"Can you . . . really mean . . . that?"

She looked up into his eyes as she spoke.

In that moment they were joined by an indivisible magnetism and it was impossible to move.

Then the Earl said:

"I thought your sister beautiful and so she is. But it is entirely a surface beauty which will fade when she grows older as a flower fades once it has come to full bloom. You are different."

"In what . . . way?"

"Your beauty comes from your heart, your soul, and perhaps from the Power that you believe will help us when we need it most."

He made a sound that was half a laugh and half a groan as he added:

"My darling, if ever we needed that Power, we need it now! For how else can you be mine, as I want you to be?"

"You want me . . . you really . . . want me?"

"Ever since we came on this journey," the Earl said, "I have been wondering how I could live without you."

He spoke quite simply and yet it seemed to Lydia

as if his voice rang out like a clarion call and she knew her whole being leapt in response.

"I . . . love you!" she said. "You know I would do anything you . . . asked me to do."

"That is what I thought you would say," the Earl replied, "but how, my precious, could I ask you to do anything so dishonourable as to run away with me, and offend against the code of behaviour in which you and I have been brought up?"

He gave a deep sigh before he said:

"I have given my word as a gentleman that I will marry your sister. God alone knows how I can tell her that I am so deeply in love with you that marriage to her is impossible!"

"No, no! You cannot do that!"

Lydia felt as she spoke that she was throwing away her only chance of happiness and closing the gates of Heaven for ever.

But she knew that to the Earl his word of honour was as sacred as if he had already made his marriage vows, and it would be wrong of her to encourage him to break his engagement or even allow him to think it was possible.

It flashed through her mind that as he was of such social importance, and so many people admired him as a sportsman, he could only behave honourably, however much he suffered in doing so.

As if he was following what she was thinking the Earl suddenly cried:

"I cannot lose you! I cannot!"

At the same time he pulled her against him and was kissing her again; kissing her with hard possessive, passionate kisses, as if he was forcing her to become his.

Only as he became aware of his own violent desire for her and felt she responded to him did he raise his head to say in a different voice but still a little unsteadily:

"I suppose if I behaved properly, I would go to join the rest of our boat-crew, and leave you here until somebody arrives to rescue us."

Lydia gave a little cry.

"N–no . . . please do not . . . leave me. I want to be with you . . . and I want to feel . . . safe in your . . . arms."

Her voice stumbled over the last words and the Earl said:

"That is what I want too, my precious. While I know I am behaving very reprehensibly, it is something I cannot help."

"For the moment," Lydia said in a low voice, "we are . . . alone and nobody . . . except the birds . . . will know . . . how we behave."

The Earl smiled, then he said:

"My darling, you have just been telling me how honourable I must be."

"I know," Lydia agreed, "but . . . love seems to sweep away everything but that I am close to you . . . and you . . . care for me."

"'Care' is a very inadequate word to describe what I feel," the Earl said in a low voice, "but I have to think of you and actually, my precious one, I am not protecting you from the gossip of a world who cannot see us, but from myself!"

She looked up at him and he knew because of her

innocence she did not understand what he was saying.

She was so different from all the other women he had ever known and he knew that what he felt for her was not only a burning desire to make her his, but also because of her purity, a reverence.

"I adore you," he said, "and I promise you, my darling, that all I want to do is look after you and protect you."

"That is why you must...stay with me," Lydia said quickly. "Supposing there are...Hawaiian warriors like the ones who...killed Captain Cook lurking in the jungle and who if I were...alone would...kill me?"

The Earl thought she looked so lovely as she spoke that any man who saw her would not want to kill her, but would have a very different idea of what he wanted to do.

Yet he knew that he had to control himself and do nothing to frighten or upset her.

"Very well," he said. "We will stay here, but darling, when you look back on this adventure it will remain something very precious in your memory, and you will know that you drove me very hard."

Because she did not understand, Lydia replied:

"Whatever happens in the future...I shall always know that this was the most wonderful...glorious moment of my...life...and yet I thought when you...kissed me it was something which was inevitable and had perhaps been planned thousands of years before...we were born."

"I am sure that is true," the Earl smiled, "and I have been searching for you all those thousands of years, only to be disappointed."

Then he was kissing her again, kissing her at first gently, then more fiercely and demandingly until when they were both breathless, Lydia hid her face against his shoulder and said in a very small voice:

"We can . . . only go on . . . hoping."

"Hoping for what?" the Earl asked bitterly. "That Heloise will die before you? That she was drowned last night at sea? Those things, my darling, do not happen except in story books. In real life we have to face the truth, that I am committed for life!"

"We might . . . see each . . . other from . . . time to time," Lydia faltered.

"How could I bear that?" the Earl asked. "How can I go through life living at the Abbey, knowing you are not far away, but I cannot see you?"

He paused before he went on:

"How can I go out hunting without searching the field to see if you are there? How can I listen to my wife speak of you and feel every time she says your name that it is as if a dagger had been plunged into my body, drawing my very life-blood?"

He spoke so violently that Lydia gave a little cry.

"You must try not to feel like that," she said, "but just believe that our love is great enough to make us behave as we . . . should do until perhaps one day . . . by the mercy of God . . . we can be . . . together."

"Do you really believe that?" the Earl asked. "In my experience God is not often merciful in matters which concern the heart."

"That is not true," Lydia said quickly, "and perhaps I am being prophetic when I say that because I love you with every breath I draw, and because I feel I am part of you, one day we will be together."

He looked down at her and there was a tenderness in his eyes she had never seen before.

"Only you, my precious love, could believe that," he said, "but because I worship you and am prepared to accept everything you tell me, I shall pray that some day God will remember us."

The way he spoke was so moving that Lydia felt the tears come into her eyes.

As she looked up at him he thought it would be impossible for any woman to look more lovely and so spiritual that her face was like a light shining in the darkness.

He took one of her hands in his, kissed it and said:

"I adore you! But now, because I must look after you I am going to find you something to eat. You can call it breakfast, if you like, but I feel we are both hungry."

"Something to . . . eat?" Lydia repeated.

She looked around her then gave a little laugh.

"Yes, I am sure there must be plenty in this magical Paradise, and now that you speak of it, I am hungry."

"If I was looking after you properly, I should have thought of it before," the Earl said. "There are sure to be bananas somewhere, and unless I am mistaken guavas are the most common fruit in the islands."

Lydia gave a laugh and rose to her feet.

"Let us go to find them," she said.

They moved into the thick vegetation and found some guavas quite easily.

Her books had told her that they were tangy but

juicy and quenched the thirst.

After that they found quite a number of ripe berries which were delicious and then the Earl discovered a papaya which they divided between them, using a sharp stone as a knife.

When they had finished and had washed their fingers in the sea Lydia said:

"I am sure if we had some matches and could make a fire I could find some birds' eggs and cook you a delicious meal."

The Earl laughed.

"I would adore to live on a desert island with you, my darling. At the same time I feel if there were many storms like last night's, we would find it very cold, however close I held you in my arms."

She blushed at the way he spoke, then once again was conscious that her nightgown, although it was made of lawn, was very revealing.

She was so used to not thinking about herself that it was really only in that moment that Lydia became aware that the Earl's eyes were on the curves of her breasts, or that against the sunlight he could see every contour of her body.

Because she loved him so overwhelmingly it did not seem to matter, and she had only to look into his eyes to move closer to him and lift her lips to his, waiting for him to kiss her.

"I love you!" he said, pulling her almost roughly against him. "It has been an agony I hope never to experience again to be acutely conscious of you every minute of every hour we have been on this journey, and at the same time to know that it would be most

127

dishonourable to let you know what I was feeling."

"I was so . . . afraid that you would . . . guess how much I . . . loved you."

"I found it impossible to think of anything else when you were near me."

"How was I to know that?"

She was thinking of how it had hurt her when she imagined he was making love to Heloise, and how she had sat alone in her cabin on the ship and in her bedroom on the train, trying to think of other things.

"How could we really believe we could do without each other for the rest of our lives?" the Earl asked.

He looked out to sea. Then he said:

"In a short time I am quite certain we shall be rescued. They will be coming from Honolulu to search for all the missing travellers on the ship."

"I want to stay . . . here with . . . you for . . . ever and ever!"

"I wonder how soon you would become bored?"

"Never . . . as long as I was . . . with you."

The Earl did not speak, but she knew he felt the same. Then he said:

"Why should we crucify ourselves? Come away with me! We will take my yacht and go round the world, and when we come back people will have a great number of other scandals to talk about and we shall have been forgotten."

Lydia smiled.

"If you were any other man that would be true," she said, "but you are different. You are you—a hero, a leader. How could I rob you of that and, I am certain, cause great harm not only to Heloise, but to a great number of other people who admire you?"

The Earl took his arms from her and walked away two paces, then back again.

"That is what I might expect you to say," he said. "At the same time, I feel trapped! No wild animal in a cage ever wanted to break out of it as violently as I wish to do!"

She knew as he spoke that he was finding it intolerable to be constrained into doing anything against his will and that his whole being rebelled against being imprisoned by a marriage that would never be anything but a farce.

Then because she could not bear his unhappiness, she ran towards him and put her arms round his neck.

"I love you!" she said. "I love you so much that I would kill myself rather than allow you to suffer because of me."

"You are not to say such things," he rebuked her angrily.

"It is true!" she insisted, "and because I love you I will not spoil anything about you, or your honour. How could I endure it if people sneered at you or said you had betrayed your own image?"

The Earl did not reply, he merely kissed her and now his lips were not passionate, but tender and gentle.

She knew he understood what she was saying and that although it broke his heart, he would abide by it.

Then as with an effort they took their eyes from each other and automatically looked out to sea, they saw a boat coming towards the shore.

They were being rescued from a Heaven of happiness they might never find again.

chapter six

LYDIA saw there were five men in the boat, one of them a Naval Officer, and she said hastily:

"I cannot let . . . them see me . . . like this."

"No, of course not," the Earl agreed. "Go and hide in the bushes, and I will see if they have something with which you can cover yourself."

She ran away from him across the sand and into the thick jungle of flowering shrubs.

The Earl walked to the edge of the sea, and saw coming towards them one of the long thin Hawaiian boats being rowed by four men and with the Naval Officer in the stern directing them.

As they rowed along the shore-line he was looking searchingly among the trees and in the bays, and the Earl felt sure that he was seeking for him.

He waved and the boat instantly pulled towards him.

As soon as it came to rest on the sand two of the oarsmen jumped out and dragged its bow out of the water.

The Naval Officer saluted.

"I am delighted to find you, My Lord," he said. "We were extremely worried when we realised last night you were missing."

He drew nearer as he spoke and the Earl asked:

"What has happened?"

"The Captain and a dozen of the crew stayed aboard the Ship to try to put out the fire. They managed it eventually, but one stoker lost his life and three seamen were badly burned."

"It is out!" the Earl exclaimed. "That is good news!"

"We are all delighted, My Lord, as you can imagine," the Naval Officer said. "Your valet and Sir Robert's have already gone back on board to try to collect Your Lordship's luggage which we think will be unharmed, as the fire was prevented from reaching that part of the ship."

The Earl smiled.

"I am glad, for at the moment I feel somewhat inadequately clothed!

The Officer looked down in the boat.

"I have brought some blankets and bandages with me in case Your Lordship was injured," he said, "but stupidly I did not think of clothes."

He paused before he went on:

"Your Lordship will not think it impertinent if I offer you my coat? And as the King's representatives will be waiting for you when we return, perhaps you would also accept my shoes."

The Earl laughed.

"Thank you, I am very grateful."

The Officer who was a young Lieutenant took off his white coat and helped the Earl into it.

They were about the same size and it was therefore not a bad fit. As he removed his shoes the Earl said:

"I think a bandage also is what I need."

"You are injured?" the Lieutenant asked quickly.

The Earl shook his head.

"No, but I could use it to cover my neck."

The Lieutenant handed him a box in which there was a number of bandages of all sizes.

They were made from strips of white linen and the Earl took the widest of them and wound it round his neck in the same way that he would have worn a stock out hunting.

"Now," he said as he tucked the ends into the coat, "I would like a blanket for Miss Westbury."

"I thought I saw her here when I first sighted you," the Lieutenant exclaimed.

"As she is as inadequately clothed as I was, you will understand that she is somewhat embarrassed."

The Lieutenant lifted a white blanket from the boat and the Earl took it from him and started to walk across the sand to where Lydia was hiding.

While the Earl was talking to their rescuers Lydia had been looking around her at the beauty of the shrubs and trees, thinking she must imprint them on her mind because she would never come here again.

It was an agony to think she would never again see the sunlight percolating through the thick trees overhead, or the exquisite blossom of the shrubs.

Then, while she was looking around her, thinking that if she were an artist she would paint a picture of it so that she could never forget it, she saw what she had longed to see.

For a moment she thought it was a blossom, but then she realised that it was the elusive Hawaiian Honeycreeper, which she had read about as being the most colourful of the song-birds on the islands.

It looked exactly as she had expected it would, with its crimson plumage and long, curved beak which enabled it to dip deep into the tubular flowers to reach their nectar.

Lydia stood very still, and the Honeycreeper looked at her with inquisitive eyes before, so swiftly that she could hardly follow its flight, it vanished upwards among the leaves into the sunshine.

Because it was so beautiful, she felt perhaps it was an omen of good luck.

Because she had seen it so unexpectedly, she would go on hoping, as she had told the Earl she would, that one day they would be together.

The Earl, with the blanket over his arm, pushed his way through the bushes until he found Lydia.

She was standing very still with her head thrown back, looking up into the tree through which the Honeycreeper had flown away.

In her white nightgown which clung to her slight figure, revealing rather than concealing her beauty, he thought she looked like the goddess Aphrodite, and he could almost believe there was a Divine Light exuding from her.

Then as if she realised he was there she turned around and the radiance in her eyes was so compelling that for a moment the Earl could not move, but could only look at her.

He thought then that it was impossible that any woman could be more lovely.

Then knowing they were out of sight of their rescuers, he held out his arms, and with a little cry of joy Lydia threw herself against him.

"I love you!" he said. "In fact, I have a very good mind to tell the boat to go away and come back tomorrow!"

"That is what I would like," Lydia answered, "but you would miss the Coronation."

She gave a little cry.

"The Coronation! It is today! You must not be late for it!"

The Earl's lips twisted wryly.

"We are about to leave our dream-island," he said, "and step back into the Social world which is waiting to gobble us up."

"I know," Lydia said unhappily, "but this is why you came to Honolulu, and I must not do anything to distract you from your duty."

The Earl did not answer. He merely kissed her.

Then he wrapped the white blanket around her shoulders and stood back for a moment to look at her.

"You look like a Saint!" he exclaimed. "I feel I ought to kneel at your feet and burn a candle to you!"

"You are not to speak like that," Lydia cried. "I do not feel at all good or holy at the moment. I only know I love you and however wrong it may be, I shall love you all my life!"

The Earl kissed her again.

Then because there was nothing more to say to

each other, he took her by the hand and drew her through the scented blossoms out onto the sandy beach.

She walked carefully with her bare feet, and when she reached the boat she realised that the sailors and the Officer were looking at her with admiration.

She had in fact, no idea how lovely she looked with her hair waving on each side of her face and falling over her shoulders onto the blanket.

The sunshine seemed to be reflected in the light of her eyes and, as the Earl had seen, because her love had lifted her spiritually into a Heaven of happiness she had a radiance that had something holy about it.

The Lieutenant helped her into the boat while the Earl paused to put on his white shoes which he had left on the sand.

Then the Earl joined Lydia and they sat side by side as the Hawaiian oarsmen carried them to Honolulu at a tremendous speed.

They seemed literally to shoot like an arrow through the calm water and more quickly than they had expected the roofs of the town were in sight and they could see a long stretch of golden beach with palm-trees growing down to the water's edge.

Behind were the majestic Koolau mountains.

Sheer walls of green and brown rock all covered with strange but beautiful vegetation, they were quite different from anything Lydia had expected.

In fact, the dazzling green of the mountains, the blue of the sea, and the gold of the beaches made her know that she had been right when she had thought Honolulu would be exactly like a fairy-story.

She was glad that she had seen it for the first time with the Earl.

Although he did not speak she knew that he was feeling as she was, that it was still part of their island Paradise, and if it was a fairy-story it must somehow have a happy ending.

As the Lieutenant brought the boat into a place where she could see a large number of people waiting for them Lydia suddenly felt shy.

She was acutely conscious that if the Earl looked more or less like his usual self in his borrowed clothes, she must look very strange in nothing but her night-gown and a blanket.

As if once again the Earl knew what she was thinking he said quietly:

"Do not worry. Leave everything to me."

She gave him a little smile knowing that was all she wanted to do for ever and ever.

As the boat pulled up beside a small wooden jetty the Earl stepped out first, and immediately a pretty girl in Hawaiian dress came forward with a garland of flowers in her hand which Lydia knew was known as a *Lei*.

She placed it round his neck, then kissed his cheek.

Leis were used originally as offerings to the gods, but now she was aware it was a gesture of love and a symbol of welcome.

Then several Hawaiians in Military uniform bowed to the Earl and presented themselves as representatives of the King.

Only when he had shaken hands with them did the Earl turn back to hold out his hand to Lydia and draw her beside him.

"As I expect you know," he said, "Miss Westbury was with me when our boat was unfortunately swamped by the waves. She has been very brave, but it has been a dramatic experience, and I want to take her immediately to wherever she is staying with her father."

A *Lei* was placed round Lydia's neck and they were then taken to an open carriage which had the Royal Insignia on it.

Having thanked the Lieutenant and arranged about the return of his clothes, the Earl helped Lydia into the carriage and sat beside her while two Hawaiian Officers sat opposite them.

"You were unfortunate, My Lord," one of them who was a General said, in good English, "that your boat was over-turned."

"Was ours the only one?" the Earl enquired.

"The others all reached here safely last night," the General replied, "and no member of the crew was unaccounted for except for those who have been rescued at the same time as yourself."

"I am extremely glad about that," the Earl said, "and also that the fire has been extinguished in *HMS Victorious*."

"His Majesty was pleased to hear the good news," the General replied, "and he is My Lord, looking forward to welcoming you at the Palace."

He paused and before the Earl could ask the question he added:

"That is where Your Lordship will be staying, while Sir Robert Westbury and his two daughters will be at the British Consulate with Mr. Wodehouse."

The Earl thought that was what he might have expected, and a few minutes later the horses turned in through two white gates and Lydia saw in front of them an attractive low-storeyed house with a flag-pole on which flew the Union Jack.

As the carriage drew to a standstill the Earl said to the General:

"As I know we are pressed for time, General, and the King will be getting ready for the Coronation which I think I am right in saying is at midday, I will just hand Miss Westbury over to her father, then rejoin you."

Lydia was aware that he was saying tactfully that it would be best for the Hawaiians to stay in the carriage.

She gave them a shy smile when they said goodbye to her and the Earl helped her out and up the steps of the British Consulate.

There was a large cool hall and a servant led them across it and opened the door of what Lydia thought was the Drawing-Room.

Sitting in front of an open window was her father and two other people who she realised must be the British Consul and his wife.

Good-looking with a large moustache, the British Consul sprang to his feet at their entrance exclaiming:

"They have found you, My Lord! Thank God for that!"

He hurried forward, his hand outstretched, and the Earl said:

"We are safe Mr. Wodehouse but of course a little shaken by our unfortunate experience, as you can understand."

"We were deeply perturbed when you did not arrive last night, and of course, what made it worse, Miss Westbury was also missing."

Lydia smiled and moved towards her father.

"I am back safely, Papa," she said, "and I am sorry if you have been worried."

"Very worried!" Sir Robert answered.

As he spoke the door burst open and Heloise came into the room.

Surprisingly, she was not fully dressed but was wearing a light muslin wrap ruched and trimmed with lace over her petticoats, her hair hung down her back and was tied with a bow of blue satin ribbon.

She swept towards them exclaiming in a loud voice as she did so:

"I heard you were back! I am surprised it should have taken so long to find you!"

She passed the Earl to confront Lydia where she stood beside her father and went on:

"Where have you been and what have you been doing? You had no right to hang back deliberately instead of getting into the boat with me and Papa!"

"I did not do . . . that," Lydia replied in a low voice.

She felt embarrassed that Heloise should be shouting at her in front of the Earl in the hard voice she used when they were alone.

"Do not lie!" Heloise stormed. "You lingered behind so that you should not accompany me as you ought to have done, but travel in another boat with Hunter!"

"That . . . is not . . . true!"

"You lie! You lie!" Heloise shouted. "And what have you been doing all night instead of getting here as everybody else managed to do?"

She was working herself up into one of her passions, and now as if she acted impulsively and without

140

thinking she raised her hand intending to slap Lydia across the face.

It was something she often did at home, but as Lydia instinctively moved her head to avoid the blow Heloise hit her instead on the forehead where she had been bruised the night before.

It was so painful and because she was taken by surprise and encumbered by the blackout Lydia fell back onto the sofa which was just behind her.

For a moment there was only darkness and she did not hear what was happening:

"Heloise . . . !" Sir Robert exclaimed sharply.

Before he could say any more the Earl was beside her.

"Stop!" he commanded. "Stop that immediately!"

At the stern interruption Heloise turned her attention from her sister to him.

"Do not give me orders!" she raged. "You have behaved abominably and you should be ashamed of yourself! Instead of looking after me and protecting me, you stayed behind with my sister and spent the night with her!"

Her voice rose to a shrill shriek as she added:

"I know all about your reputation, Hunter, and the way you behave with other women, but I thought you would cease your philandering tricks, at least until we were married!"

The Earl stood very still, his eyes on Heloise.

He was thinking that when she was in a rage and her face was contorted with anger she lost all her beauty and became positively ugly.

"I am disgusted by you, do you hear?" Heloise

went on as he did not speak.

"Really, Heloise," Sir Robert intervened, "you cannot talk in that way to the man you are going to marry!"

"Marry?"

Heloise made the word vibrate around the room as she repeated it shrilly.

"Marry! I would not marry such a rake and lecher if he was the last man in the world!"

There was only a second's silence before the Earl said quietly but clearly:

"In which case I can only accept that you have terminated our engagement and our marriage will not now take place!"

He looked towards Mrs. Wodehouse, the Consul's wife who was sitting as if turned to stone by the scene taking place in front of her.

He bowed to her politely and said:

"I hope you will excuse me, but I understand His Majesty is waiting impatiently for my arrival at the Palace."

He then walked from the room with great dignity, and only as the door closed quietly behind him did Sir Robert and the Consul find their breath.

Then Mr. Wodehouse picked Lydia up from the sofa and carried her across the room while his wife opened the door for him to take her slowly up the stairs.

As he did so Lydia opened her eyes and had a glimpse through the open door of the Earl driving away in the Royal carriage.

The pain of the blow on her head had made her faint and although she had heard as if from a distance her sister's voice shrieking hysterically, she had not understood what she was saying.

Now she told herself that the Earl was driving out of her life. The thought that she was losing him for ever was more agonising than anything she could suffer physically and she closed her eyes again.

Mr. Wodehouse took her into a bedroom where there were two Hawaiian maid-servants waiting for her arrival.

He put her gently down on the bed and said to the elder of the two:

"Look after Miss Westbury. Do not leave her alone, and do not let anybody disturb her."

"Yes, that is right," Mrs. Wodehouse said who had followed her husband. "Nobody is to disturb her until she has slept. She is very tired. But bring her something to eat and drink, as I am sure she must be hungry."

She then went from the room with her husband following her and outside she said to the maid who had opened the door:

"Make quite certain no one goes near Miss Westbury until she wakes."

"I keep watch, Mistress," the girl replied.

As husband and wife walked down the stairs Mr. Wodehouse said:

"I hope your orders are carried out, Mary. That ghastly girl must not be allowed to upset her sister more than she has done already."

"I could not have believed that any lady could behave in such a disgraceful manner!" Mrs. Wodehouse answered. "If you ask me, James, the Earl is well rid of her!"

Mr. Wodehouse smiled.

"That is exactly what I thought myself."

Left alone in the Drawing-Room Sir Robert said
to Heloise:

"Are you mad? How could you be so rude to Royston?"

Heloise was actually feeling somewhat abashed by
the way first the Earl, then everybody else had disappeared, but she tossed her head defiantly.

"You know as well as I do, Papa," she replied,
"that he should have come with us last night, and
taken care of me!"

"You were quite safe," Sir Robert replied.

"He was not to know that! And how dare he spend
the night alone with Lydia, and without a chaperon?"

Sir Robert laughed, but there was no humour in
the sound.

"I do not suppose they chose to be capsized in a
stormy sea," he replied. "In fact, Mr. Wodehouse was
saying, if you had listened, that they were extremely
fortunate not to have been drowned."

"If they had been with us they would have been
perfectly all right, as we were," Heloise objected.

Sir Robert was too tactful to remind his daughter
that she had behaved hysterically all the time they
were in the boat, clinging to him convulsively and
reiterating over and over again that they would die.

Instead he said dryly:

"If you have lost Royston I think I shall wring your
neck! You are not likely to give me another son-in-
law who is so distinguished and so rich."

"Oh, he will soon be back," Heloise said compla-

cently, "and will apologise abjectly to me for his neglect which is something I am not used to."

"Oh, for Heaven's sake, Heloise," Sir Robert said
crossly, "try to understand that Royston has more
women running after him than he has horses, which
is saying a great deal, and as you have been stupid
enough to throw him over, he is not likely to come
crawling back!"

"You are quite wrong—you will see!" Heloise retorted airily. "Now I must go to get ready for the
Coronation, and Lydia must do my hair."

She walked up the stairs, but when she tried to go
into Lydia's room the Hawaiian housemaid stood in
front of the door and refused to let her enter.

When Heloise raged at her and insisted she must
speak to her sister, the other maid went to fetch Mrs.
Wodehouse who hurried up the stairs and said:

"I cannot believe, Miss Westbury, that you are not
aware that your sister is in a delicate state of health
after her terrible experience of last night. Besides
which, when you struck her she fainted."

There was a note of condemnation in Mrs. Wodehouse's voice which for once made Heloise ashamed
of the way she had acted.

"I can hardly go to the Coronation with my hair
as it is at the moment!" she replied. "Perhaps you
could send for a Hair-dresser."

"I think it unlikely that one will be available at
such short notice," Mrs. Wodehouse replied, "but my
head maid is very skilful with hair, and all the Hawaiian girls have theirs beautifully arranged at Fes-
tivals."

There was nothing Heloise could do therefore but

accept the services of the Hawaiian maid, who in fact, arranged her hair very prettily.

Heloise however made it perfectly clear that she would expect Lydia to wait on her before the Ball which was to take place that night.

"When you see my sister," she said coldly when she was dressed and ready to leave, "will you please inform her that I expect her to be up by the time I return."

"I will see if I consider her well enough to rise," Mrs. Wodehouse replied. "Otherwise, Miss Westbury, I am afraid you will have to manage without her."

Just after Lydia's arrival with the Earl the luggage had been brought to the house, having been retrieved from *HMS Victorious*.

Heloise made a great fuss over which gown she was to wear but thanks to Lydia's forethought in listing what was in every trunk, everything she required was found comparatively easily.

Mrs. Wodehouse did not miss the fact that while Heloise had more than a dozen trunks Lydia had only one, and after what she had seen and heard in the Drawing-Room her kind heart went out to somebody who she thought, was being extremely badly treated by her relatives.

When she was driving with her husband to the Royal Pavilion especially built for the Coronation she said to him:

"I cannot understand Sir Robert treating one of his daughters so differently from the other, and I am already convinced in my mind that poor little Cinderella who is the elder, is much the nicer of the two."

"I think the same," Mr. Wodehouse said, "but it is no use your interfering, my dear, you will get no thanks for it."

It was not surprising that Lydia lying in bed feeling limp and listless, was depressed at missing the Coronation Ceremony.

When the King had decided to have a Coronation such as no King of Hawaii had ever had before, he ordered a Royal Pavilion to be built in front of Iolani Palace.

A covered amphitheatre surrounded it on three sides and provided seating for thousands of spectators.

Octagonal, the domed pavilion symbolised the Crown and its eight Grecian columns represented the eight uninhabited islands of the Hawaiian Kingdom.

Inside the Royal Pavilion the Chief Justice of the Kingdom placed the Royal Mantle—the large feather cloak of Kamehameha I—on the King's shoulders, and handed him a Royal Sceptre.

The Princess Poomaikelani, his sister-in-law, presented him with a *pulo' ulo'u Rapu* stick and a whale tooth pendant suspended from a necklace of woven human hair.

Besides this he also received a Royal feather standard.

The Coronation's greatest moment however came when one of the Princes stepped forward with the crowns which had been made in England.

As the choir sang: *"Almighty Father! We do Bring Gold and Gems for the King,"* King Kalakaua took his crown, placed it on his head, then placed a smaller similar crown on the head of Queen Kapiolani.

The choir sang: *"Cry out O Isles with Joy!"*

147

Cannons on land and at sea fired a salute after which the Royal Hawaiian Band played a spirited *Coronation March*.

Then the general festivities started and Sir Robert thought that King Kalakaua certainly lived up to his reputation as a 'Merry Monarch.'

The whole populace was dressed in their best and Honolulu seemed to be turned into a Fun-Fair of beautiful girls dancing, every kind of side-show and sport taking place as well as the beach being crowded with surf-bathers.

The gaiety of it was so irresistible that the Earl who had been treated as a Royal Personage kept thinking how much Lydia would have enjoyed it.

He had a special place in the Pavilion, to which he had been escorted by the Lord Chamberlain, and until he was seated everybody stood.

The King singled him out for a special greeting so that the people could understand that he was embracing the Queen of England in the personage of the Earl.

At the Royal Banquet which followed the Coronation the Earl was given the Seat of Honour.

Heloise was seated a long way away from him. He deliberately did not look in her direction and there was no question of either her or Sir Robert speaking to him while the ceremony and the banquet was taking place.

On the way back to the British Consulate Heloise grumbled all the way.

"You would think, Papa," she said, "after his disgraceful behaviour that Hunter would have made some effort to speak to me and apologise."

"You will be lucky if he comes near you!" Sir Robert replied.

He was actually very perturbed by the way in which Heloise had behaved.

Although it was something which he and Lydia were used to and they seldom took seriously anything she said when she was in a tantrum he was sensible enough to be aware that to the Earl it must have been an unpleasant 'eye-opener.'

Then because he always tried to avoid unpleasant facts, Sir Robert told himself he was quite certain that the Earl was deeply in love with Heloise and bemused by her beauty.

He would therefore forgive her, even though such a vulgar exhibition should never have taken place in front of the British Consul and his wife.

There was however no point in saying so, and taking the line of least resistance Sir Robert said;

"I am sure tonight you will be dancing with Royston at the Ball. But do not expect him to grovel because no man likes doing that!"

Heloise did not answer.

She merely swept into the house and told the servant that she was going to her room to rest and wanted her sister to come to her immediately.

She, however, received a message from Mrs. Wodehouse saying that Lydia was still asleep and a maid would prepare her bath in an hour's time.

Heloise was therefore forced to explain to a strange maid how to undo her gown and to find in her innumerable trunks the one she intended to wear at the Palace.

* * *

Lydia awoke feeling she had slept for a very long time and finding she had now recovered from the strain and fatigue she had felt when she got into bed.

She had eaten what the maids had brought her but she was hardly aware of what she was doing.

Then she had drifted away into a delicious sleep in which she thought the Earl's arms were around her, his lips were near to hers, and she could hear his deep voice saying that he loved her.

"I love you!" she found herself whispering as she opened her eyes.

As she did so she realised that the sun was sinking low over the sea and the sky was a vision of loveliness.

'I have missed the whole day!' she thought with a little pang. 'How could I have done anything so stupid when I can sleep at home?'

However she felt immeasurably better, and because it was difficult to think of the Coronation or anything else except the Earl, she knew the only thing that mattered was that she should see him again.

Then she remembered vaguely hearing Heloise screaming at her. She had seen him drive away and thought he was going out of her life for ever.

She felt the pain of it stab through her and told herself severely she would have to be sensible.

What had happened on the island where they had been marooned was something which would never happen again.

It had been so perfect, so exquisite, such an ecstatic memory, that nothing must ever spoil it.

'It is in my heart and in his,' she thought, 'and will be ours for all eternity.'

She got out of bed and started to dress herself, thinking all the time of the Earl and finding it extraordinary that while she had been with him on the island wearing nothing but a nightgown she had not felt shy.

She had not been embarrassed until the Hawaiian boat had arrived to rescue them.

She knew the explanation was that she had felt she belonged to him and therefore everything they did together was right and perfect.

"I love him! I love him!" she said to the sunset, and felt that the crimson and gold wonder of it brought her the light of hope.

Because she was not certain if she was to be allowed to go to the Ball tonight, although she knew her father had intended taking her to the Coronation, she merely put on one of her simple white evening dresses which was less elaborate than any gown she would have worn to attend the Ball.

She quickly arranged her hair at the back of her head and opened the door of her bedroom.

The maid-servant outside in the passage smiled at her and said;

"You wake, Lady. That good! Why you not call?"

"I managed by myself, thank you," Lydia replied. "Will you show me the way to my sister's bedroom?"

The maid led her across the landing and as she went in she saw that Heloise was dressing herself and looking exceedingly sulky.

"Can I help you?" Lydia asked.

"It is about time you did!" Heloise answered. "And you will have to hurry! Papa sent a message to say he will be leaving in half-an-hour."

"In half-an-hour?" Lydia exclaimed. "Where is Papa? I want to ask him if I am to come with you."

"Come with us?" Heloise questioned. "Do you think I would want you there after the way you behaved? You will do my hair and help me dress, then stay here and try to behave yourself until we get back!"

The way she spoke was so rude and so peremptory that Lydia was quite certain that if she asked her father he would say she was not to upset Heloise and must therefore stay behind.

She was disappointed.

At the same time, knowing it was what she might have expected would happen, she merely arranged Heloise's hair in silence, helped her into her gown, and fastened round her neck the jewels that had belonged to her mother.

Then without saying 'thank you,' Heloise swept towards the door and down the stairs with Lydia following her.

Her father looking very smart and wearing his decorations on his evening-coat was waiting in the hall.

As Heloise appeared he pulled out his watch and said:

"Come along! Come along! We are late! I have already had to apologise to our host and hostess, because we are travelling with them in their carriage."

As he spoke Mr. and Mrs. Wodehouse came from the Drawing-Room.

They looked at Lydia as she descended the last steps of the staircase and Mrs. Wodehouse asked:

"Are you feeling better, my dear?"

"Yes, thank you," Lydia replied. "You have been

so very kind, and I am exceedingly grateful for all you have done for me."

"It has been a pleasure," Mrs. Wodehouse said warmly, "and now I hope you will enjoy the Ball."

"It is very kind of you," Lydia said, "but if it will be no trouble, I think I had better...stay here."

She glanced nervously at her sister as she spoke and almost as if she had asked the question Heloise said:

"My sister is too tired and exhausted to attend any Ball!"

As she spoke she handed the wrap she was carrying on her arm to her father who put it round her shoulders.

"You had better go to bed, Lydia," she added. "I will wake you when I come back so that you can undo my gown."

Mrs. Wodehouse looked from one girl to the other, then said:

"I think it is very disappointing for Miss Lydia, having missed the Coronation today, now to miss the Ball. I suggest she comes with us, at least for a little time. After all, it is almost a Royal Command!"

As she spoke Lydia saw the anger in Heloise's eyes and quickly put her hand on Mrs. Wodehouse's arm.

"It is better if I stay behind," she said in a low voice, "but I hope it will be no trouble to your household."

Her fingers told Mrs. Wodehouse better than what she said that it would be a mistake to argue.

But she gave Heloise a hard look as she walked ahead of her towards the front door pausing to say to the servant who was seeing them out:

"Miss Westbury is staying behind, look after her and give her something to eat before you all join the festivities as you have been told you may do."

"We do that, Mistress," the servant said with a smile.

Then the Wodehouses, Sir Robert and Heloise all got into the closed carriage that was waiting for them and drove off.

Lydia watched them go, then she went into the Drawing-Room to stand looking out into the garden which lay on one side of the house, while there was a view of the sea on the other.

She watched the sunset, feeling that she was again on the island where the Earl had kissed her and told her he loved her.

"An Island of Love," she whispered in her heart and knew she would never forget.

The servants came in to tell Lydia there was a meal waiting for her in the Dining-Room.

She sat alone at the large table where the British Consul and his wife entertained their guests.

She did not really envy Heloise at the Ball, except for thinking how delightful and interesting it would be if she could sit next to the Earl and hear him talking to her.

It would not be about themselves since they were in public, but about Hawaii and its long, complicated but exciting history.

When the simple meal was finished she went back into the Drawing-Room, not feeling tired enough to go to bed but reliving her own love-story, which perhaps would never have another chapter.

Now the sun had sunk in a blaze of glory and with the swiftness with which the night came in the tropics the stars were coming out overhead.

There was the same moon that had shone on them last night, but the sea beneath it was calm and there were no waves except ripples at the edge of the sand.

It seemed impossible that the scene had been so violent and dramatic only the night before.

Now as the moonlight turned the ocean to silver and the palm-trees were silhouetted against the stars, Lydia felt her whole spirit was uplifted by beauty and love.

It made her think of the *Lei* that had been placed around her neck when she arrived as an offering of love, and she imagined that at this moment she was holding up a *Lei* towards the stars and prayed that she might know again the happiness that had been hers last night.

She was concentrating so intently on her thoughts that it was quite a shock when the door opened and a very old servant, who had obviously not gone with the rest, said:

"Gentleman see you, Lady!"

"A gentleman?" Lydia asked in surprise.

She rose to her feet realising that the room was in darkness except for the moonlight coming through the window.

Then as she went from the Drawing-Room into the hall where the lights had been lit, she saw outside the door there was a carriage and to her astonishment the Earl got out of it and came up the steps.

She ran towards him and as she reached him she saw how magnificent he was looking with the Order of the Garter across his white evening shirt and several decorations glittering with diamonds pinned to his evening-coat.

She looked up at him and he took her hand in his and said;

"I want you, darling, to come with me."

Lydia thought he had an expression in his eyes that made her think of him as she had before, as a buccaneer or a pirate.

There was also something magnificent and vibrant about him, and she thought perhaps it was because he had been enjoying the Coronation besides the fact that he was seeing her again.

"Where are you taking me?" she asked.

"There is no time for explanations," he replied. "Fetch your bonnet and something to put over your shoulders. You look very lovely, just as you are!"

She thought then he was taking her for a drive and that it was like him to be determined she should not miss everything of the festivities, and intended to show some of them to her himself.

Without saying any more she ran hastily up the stairs.

As she reached her room she wished she had worn the grand gown she had intended to wear if she had gone to the Ball.

Then she knew that in fact, the simple white one with its soft chiffon round the shoulders and the draped skirt made her look like a Grecian statue and was actually far more attractive.

'Perhaps he will think as he did on the island that I look like a Saint,' she thought.

She took her bonnet from the cupboard and realised

now that the maids must have unpacked while she was asleep.

She also found a white silk shawl that she had owned for a long time, but which was very becoming.

As it was still warm outside, she felt she would not really need it.

She tied the ribbons of her bonnet under her chin and thought that in the moonlight she looked more a violet than the brilliant hibiscus flowers that were so symbolic of Hawaii.

"I am just a little English flower," she told herself with a smile, and wondered how the Earl had escaped from Heloise.

She had taken it for granted that her sister would want to monopolise him at the Ball, so she thought that it was more exciting than anything she could imagine that he had remembered her and come to her rather than stay in the Palace where he belonged.

It was only a few minutes before she ran back down the stairs, and as she did so she saw coming along the passage to her room there were two men.

She thought it was rather strange, especially as she recognised one of them as her father's valet when she was quite certain he should have been enjoying himself in the town.

However she did not stop, but merely hurried through the front door to find the Earl waiting for her inside the carriage.

She stepped in beside him and as a footman shut them in her hands went out towards him.

"My darling! My sweet!" he said. "I have missed you, I have missed you every moment that we have been away from each other!"

"I have missed you too, except when I slept for a very long time."

"That is what I hoped you would do," he said, "and you look rested and lovelier even than you did at dawn."

"I want to believe you think that," Lydia said, "but how were you able to get away from the Palace?"

The Earl smiled.

"Everybody was concentrating on the King, and I seized my opportunity to come to you."

"It was wonderful of you! I am so happy, so very, very happy to be with you again!"

"That is what I wanted you to say," the Earl replied, "and, darling, your head is not still hurting after what happened this morning?"

Because she felt so happy Lydia could not remember what it was. Then she recalled that the Earl had seen Heloise hit her.

Because it made her feel ashamed she said quickly:

"I do not want to...talk about it...but I am quite...all right. Tell me about yourself and what happened at the Coronation."

"I kept thinking how disappointing it was that you should miss it," the Earl said. "That is why I have arranged a special Coronation of our own, just you and me."

"That sounds wonderful!" Lydia said a little breathlessly. "But what are we going to do?"

"We are going to be married!" the Earl said very quietly.

chapter seven

FOR a moment Lydia felt she could not have heard what he said correctly.

Then she asked in a halting little voice:

"D–did you say we . . . were to be . . . married?"

"Yes, darling," he answered, "we are going to be married tonight so that there can be no arguments afterwards that you do not belong to me."

"But . . . Heloise . . . ?"

"Heloise broke our engagement in front of your father and the Wodehouses," the Earl said. "I accepted it, and as far as I am concerned the whole episode is finished."

There was a hard note in his voice which instinctively made Lydia move nearer to him.

Then as she stared up at him her eyes wide and a little frightened, he said:

"Leave everything to me. Everything is arranged

159

and all you have to remember is that I love you!"

As he spoke she felt as though the whole world was lit with a glory that was indescribable.

Then as they drove along the road there were people dancing and singing with happiness, and Lydia knew her heart was doing the same.

The carriage came to a standstill.

As the Earl got out and put up his hand to help her alight she saw they were outside the stately Kawaiahao Church which she had read about in Hawaiian history.

The Earl took her by the hand and drew her up the long flight of stone steps through the Ionic columns and into the dim sanctity of the Church which was lit only by candles.

Waiting at the altar steps was a Minister.

What the Earl had said had so surprised Lydia that she felt that what was now happening must be a dream and could not be true.

And yet as they stood before the parson and he began to read the Marriage Service, she felt as if all the angels in Heaven were singing and the Church was filled with music.

The Earl made his vows with deep sincerity, while Lydia's voice was very soft. Yet she felt he knew how moved she was by what was happening.

She felt herself quiver when he put the ring on her finger.

Then as they knelt down for the blessing she thought all her prayers had been answered.

God had blessed her and the Earl in a way that was so wonderful, so perfect that she would never again, however long she lived, doubt the power of prayer, faith and hope which had brought her the man she loved.

After they had signed the Register in the Vestry and the Minister had congratulated them, they walked down the aisle and outside to where their carriage was waiting.

Only then did Lydia look at the Earl a little apprehensively, wondering if the beauty and sanctity of their marriage was to be spoilt by the row she knew must ensue when they returned and Heloise learned what had happened.

He knew what she was thinking and as they drove away he put his arms around her and said:

"You are mine, my precious, as I always meant you to be!"

"I ... I told you that you ... always win!" Lydia whispered. "But how can we tell Papa and ... Heloise what has ... happened?"

It was hard to say her sister's name, and yet she knew it must be said.

The Earl smiled.

"You do not think I would let anybody spoil our happiness at the moment?" he asked. "I have a surprise for you."

"What is it?"

"We are beginning our honeymoon in a very Royal manner."

Lydia lifted her face up to look at him curiously, and it flashed through her mind that perhaps he was taking her to the Iolani Palace.

It was a place she would like to see. At the same time she thought that anyone even the King, would be an intruder at this moment, when she wanted to be alone with the Earl.

"I waited until the King was free," the Earl said quietly, "and although His Majesty was very preoccupied with his Coronation I told him the whole story."

"You . . . told him?"

"I had a feeling, and I was right," the Earl said, "that as a 'Merry Monarch' he would understand the complications women can make in a man's life!"

He spoke teasingly and Lydia gave a little laugh as she moved closer to him.

His arms were like bands of steel as he held her against him, and she knew he was longing to kiss her but felt she must first hear his explanations.

"I told the King I was going to marry you," the Earl went on, "and he immediately suggested we should use the Royal Barge, and we could sail along the coast to a quiet bay where he has a Beach-House."

Lydia drew in her breath.

"We shall be there alone, my precious, except for the servants who will look after us, and my valet."

"It sounds very . . . wonderful!"

"It will be," the Earl promised.

He did not kiss her because by now they were moving through the centre of the town towards the Quay and the noise in the streets was almost deafening.

The crowds were dancing and celebrating the Coronation in a way that only Hawaiians can, by dancing wildly but at the same time gracefully, and exuberantly, while it sounded as if there were a dozen Bands playing and everybody was singing.

There were flags and bunting, balloons and flowers, all lit by flares and gas-lamps, and Lydia felt that her own happiness was echoed by the excited Hawaiians.

It took them a little time to reach the Quay where the King's Barge, painted red and ornamented with gold carving, was waiting.

The oarsmen were grinning as they stepped out of the carriage, and Lydia had the idea that they knew what had just taken place.

She was certain of it when a very attractive Hawaiian girl ran forward to put *Leis* of scented flowers round their necks, and there was also a bouquet of orchids for her to carry.

They stepped into the barge and the oarsmen rowed them swiftly through the water along the coast.

Now Lydia could see the whole of Honolulu lit up with lights, and it was a very beautiful sight against the Koolau mountains with the moon illuminating their peaks.

They were sitting within the covered cabin in the centre of the barge.

Lydia held tightly onto the Earl's hand, but there seemed nothing to say except that she loved him, and now they were actually married she felt as if the whole world was singing a paean of praise for them.

It took only about a quarter-of-an-hour to reach the Waikiki beach, and when the oarsmen stopped rowing Lydia could see on the other side of the deserted beach the roof of what appeared to be a small house.

She looked at the Earl and he said quietly:

"I think we will find it quite comfortable, my precious, but what is more important than anything else is that we shall be together."

She wanted to tell him that if they had to stay on the island where they had been marooned without a roof over their heads and with only the palm-trees, she would have been happy.

There were palm-trees now either side of the King's Beach-House and a number of shrubs which Lydia knew in the daytime she would find heavy with blossoms.

There was no quay but the oarsmen having brought the barge as near as possible to the shore stepped out into the water and Lydia realised they intended to carry her and the Earl to the shore.

Two of them lifted her up onto their shoulders and carried her safely onto the sand, but they did not put her down.

Instead they carried her right up to the Beach-House, and set her down just outside it where the building bordered on the sand.

Two other men carried the Earl and when he had thanked them and rewarded them for their pains they went back to the barge.

Standing with their oars pointed towards the sky they cheered loudly before they rowed away.

Only when they had done so and were disappearing back in the direction of the town did the Earl put his arm around Lydia and take her up the steps that led onto the verandah which ran the whole length of the house.

A door was open and inside there were lights but there was nobody about.

The Earl looked at Lydia for a moment, then lifted her up in his arms.

"Our first home together!" he said quietly. "For

luck I must carry you over the threshold."

She felt her heart beating excitedly because she was so close to him.

When they were inside the hut he put her down and she saw that it was not primitive as she had expected, but very comfortably furnished.

There were deep, heavily padded armchairs in what was the Sitting-Room, and also surprisingly a fireplace which could burn logs.

There was a desk and a bookcase, and the floor was covered with a thick carpet.

Lydia looked round with delight as the Earl undid the ribbons of her bonnet and threw it onto the table.

Then he put his arms around her, and very gently his lips found hers.

He kissed her with a tenderness and what she felt was almost a reverence, as if the sanctity of the Marriage Service was still in his mind.

Then his lips became more demanding, more insistent.

As if she was afraid of her own response she moved a little in his arms and said;

"Is it... true? Is it really true... that I am your... wife?"

"You are my wife," the Earl confirmed, "and I shall love and adore you for the rest of our lives together!"

"I can hardly believe it! It is so wonderful to be able to come here and be alone... but you do realise that I have nothing to wear but what I have on, and also perhaps I ought to let... Papa know what has h-happened."

There was a tremor in her voice as she spoke her

father's name and the Earl knew she was still afraid that there might be a row and was apprehensive of what her sister might do and say.

"I have thought of all that, my precious," he replied. "First of all, let me tell you that you will find in your bedroom your own clothes and an extra trunk as well."

"My . . . own clothes?" Lydia exclaimed.

She then remembered how she had seen her father's valet together with another man going towards her bedroom when she was leaving the British Consulate.

"I had your own clothes brought here," the Earl said, "and as I felt your sister would not be requiring all the gowns she had bought for her trousseau, I have stolen one of her trunks."

"I . . . I cannot believe what you are . . . saying!"

The Earl took her by the hand and drew her outside onto the verandah.

There was a seat running along it on which had been placed a number of soft cushions.

They sat down, and he put his arm around her and said:

"Why must we waste our time on such boring matters when all I want to do is kiss you? But as they have to be said, let us get them over, and then, my darling, I can tell you how much I love you."

There was a note in his voice which made her quiver and she forced herself to say:

"I must know . . . because I am . . . worried in case we have . . . done something wrong."

"We have done nothing wrong," the Earl said firmly. "Your sister told me in front of witnesses that she would not marry me if I was the last man in the world. I accepted her decision and said that as far as I was concerned our engagement was over."

Lydia wanted to say she was certain Heloise did not mean it. But there was no point in doing so, and she merely sighed as the Earl went on:

"I therefore, as I told you, spoke to the King who has lent us this house, and I left a letter for your father saying we were to be married, and I have arranged that as soon as the main part of the ceremony of the Coronation is over they will travel back to San Francisco on the Steamship *City of Sydney* in which the King started his voyage round the world. They will be quite comfortable and *The Duchess* will be waiting in San Francisco to convey them to New York."

As the Earl finished speaking Lydia gave a gasp of relief and he went on:

"After our honeymoon, although we will stay in Hawaii until we feel we can face the world again, I am taking you home by a different route. We will go by train from San Francisco to New Orleans and take a ship from there which will carry us back to England."

"It sounds . . . very exciting!" Lydia said in a small voice.

"Before we do that, however, we have one obligation to fulfill."

She looked up at him a little apprehensively and he said:

"The King very flatteringly did not want me to miss all the other excitements of his Coronation and, as I thought you might enjoy them too, I have promised that in a week's time I will take you to stay in the Palace and we will attend the horse races in Kapiolani Park."

Lydia laughed.

"I thought we would get back to the horses sooner or later!"

"Exactly!" the Earl agreed. "And the King is also anxious for me to see the Hula dancers which I think you will enjoy too."

"It sounds very exciting," Lydia murmured.

"I have also promised," the Earl answered, "that we will attend another Ball, which is one of the reasons why, my lovely wife, I stole one of your sister's trunks, knowing that you would want to dazzle everybody and I shall not have time to buy you all the clothes and jewels I intend to give you later."

"Are you . . . really saying . . . all this to me? I . . . I cannot believe what . . . I am . . . hearing!"

As she spoke she felt the tears come into her eyes and begin to run down her cheeks.

After years of being pushed on one side first by her father because she was not a boy, then by Heloise who wanted everything for herself, it seemed impossible that was now all changed as if a fairy had waved a magical wand to make all her dreams come true.

The Earl knew what she was thinking and gently held her close to him as she hid her face against his shoulder.

"I will not allow you to cry, my precious love," he said. "You are going to be happy, as we were happy last night, or rather, this morning, on our Island of Love."

"How can you be so wonderful . . . so understanding and . . . do so much for me?" Lydia asked incoherently.

"You told me I am a pirate," the Earl replied. "Therefore having captured you I am prepared to steal or plunder everything and everybody to give you what you deserve, the perfect woman who I believed did not exist, and whom it would be impossible for me to find."

"Oh, darling . . . suppose I . . . fail you?"

"You will not do that," the Earl said. "Ever since I have known you we have been so closely attuned that it would be impossible for you to do anything that I did not know about and understand, or to deceive me in any way."

He drew in his breath before he said:

"It is like finding a perfect pearl and knowing without even touching it that it is flawless. That is what you are!"

The way he spoke made Lydia's tears run even faster down her cheeks, her heart was beating in the same way.

She turned her face up to his and with his handkerchief he gently wiped away her tears.

Then his lips held hers captive and he kissed her until the whole world seemed to revolve around them dizzily.

"I want you, my darling," he said. "I have sent the servants away to their own hut which is somewhere behind us, so we are alone, which is what I have longed for and thought was impossible."

"I told you there was . . . always . . . hope," Lydia said in a quavering little voice.

"And you were right, Heart of my Heart."

She thought he was about to kiss her, but instead he drew her to her feet and they walked into the house.

The Earl passed through the Sitting-Room and opened a door which led into a bedroom of about the same size.

When she saw it Lydia could not help gasping.

'Only a King could imagine being Royal in a Beach-House!' she thought.

The huge double bed which almost filled the room was draped with embroidered curtains and on top of the canopy was a replica of a crown.

She pointed to it and gave a little laugh, and the Earl laughed too.

"It is certainly something I did not anticipate," he said.

"At least it looks . . . comfortable."

He pulled her close against him. Then he said:

"Tomorrow, or perhaps some other day while we are still here, I am going to take you back to the island on which we found ourselves last night."

She looked at him in surprise and he said:

"I wanted when I was there, more than anything I have ever wanted in my whole life, to make love to you amongst the blossoms and under the pine trees."

Lydia hid her face against his neck before she said in a whisper:

"I . . . I thought the same thing . . . and how wonderful . . . it would be!"

The Earl held her so close she could hardly breathe.

"We think the same, and we feel the same. How could our marriage be anything but perfect when we are one person—or very nearly one!"

As he spoke she felt his fingers undoing the back

of her gown and when a moment later he lifted her onto the bed she did not feel shy, but only a wild excitement that had also something spiritual about it.

She knew too a rapture which made her feel as if she was reaching for the peaks of the mountains.

Then when the Earl joined her she knew that this was the happiness she had never thought she would find, but which had come to her so unexpectedly and so suddenly that she was half-afraid it would vanish as quickly as it had come.

But as the Earl pulled her gently against him she knew he was deliberately keeping himself strictly under control, so as not to frighten her.

Because he was so gentle it made her want to cry again simply because she was so happy.

The curtains over the window were drawn back and outside she could see the sea silver in the moonlight and the stars twinkling like diamonds in the sky.

The Earl had blown out the candles by the bed and now the moon flooded into the room with a strange silver radiance that seemed to make everything mysterious and at the same time exquisitely beautiful.

"I love you!"

Lydia instinctively moved a little closer to him, feeling how strong and athletic his body was compared to the softness of hers.

"I feel as if I have fought a dozen battles," he said, "dived deep into the depths of the ocean, and stormed Heaven itself to win you!"

His lips moved over her forehead before he went on:

"When we said goodbye to each other I was desperately afraid of the future, knowing if I could not have you I would feel crippled for the rest of my life."

"My darling ... how can you ... say such ... things?"

"It is true," he replied, "but now suddenly you are mine, and I do not have to be afraid that time is passing and I shall no longer see you and shall lose you all together."

The way he spoke was very moving and Lydia said:

"We have been so lucky, so unbelievably lucky! Are you quite certain though, that people will not be ... shocked because you have ... married me?"

"I think the majority will merely imagine that they got the name wrong in the first place, and the rest, once they know you will realise I am the most fortunate man in the world and that nobody could make me a more beautiful or perfect wife."

Lydia gave a little murmur.

"I know what you are thinking, my sweet," the Earl said. "But to me you have a beauty which far exceeds that of your sister in every way, and it is the beauty for which I was always looking."

"I felt you were ... looking for something," Lydia murmured.

"First unconsciously, then consciously," he said. "I was trying to look beneath the surface to find what was inside a person and what they were really like behind their outward appearance."

Lydia knew that was what she had suspected about him.

"When I saw you," the Earl went on, "and felt you first vibrate towards me, I then began to know the beauty of your character and personality and what I suppose one might call your 'soul'!"

He kissed her cheek and said:

"You charmed me so overwhelmingly that I knew it was impossible for me to see beauty in any other woman's face."

"I ... I hope you will ... always think so, and I promise you I will ... try to do what you ... want and ... be what you ... want."

She looked at him before she said:

"But because nobody has ever ... loved me and I have ... always been kept so much in the background, I felt like a ... ghost instead of a person ... a shadow of those I was with and not really myself."

The Earl's lips moved over her skin, but he did not interrupt as she went on:

"Because you are so magnificent and so vibrant you can ... understand why I love you ... but it is impossible for me to understand why you love me ... only I do not want to fail you ... I want you to be ... proud of me ... so please ... darling ... help me ... teach me and guide me ... otherwise I shall be a ... failure."

The Earl moved so that she was lying back against the pillows and he was looking down at her. Then he said:

"When I put that blanket round you on the island and told you you looked like a Saint, I meant it. I wanted then to kneel at your feet and that is what I want to do now."

Lydia found it was impossible to breathe as he continued:

"You are good, pure and perfect, my lovely wife,

173

and because I know all these things are instinctive to you, not only will you inspire and stimulate me as you have done already, but together we will be able to help other people, and you will show me how to be worthy of those who follow my lead, either in public life or in the sporting world."

"If I could...do that I would be...very...very happy."

"That is what I intend you to be."

He looked at her for a long moment in the moonlight before he said:

"Oh, my darling, have you any idea how beautiful you are?"

Then his lips were on hers, his hand was touching her, his heart was beating against her heart, and the moonlight enveloped them with a dazzling light.

A long time later when the moon was high in the sky and there was only the sound of the waves lapping on the shore, Lydia stirred against the Earl's shoulder.

"Are you awake, my beloved?" he asked.

"I thought you must be asleep."

"I am too happy to sleep."

"I am so happy I feel we really are in...Paradise."

He smiled and said:

"And that is where we will stay because I feel, my lovely one, that our love will grow, and this is only the beginning of what we will feel for each other."

"I...love you so much," Lydia said, "I feel it is impossible to love any more...and yet I am sure you are right. There is so much more for us to find out about each other, and I am only afraid that once you...know all about me, which is not very much, you will become bored!"

The Earl laughed.

"That is very unlikely. I am in love as I have never been in love before. In fact, I have never known what love was like, until I met you."

"Then you are not...disappointed in me... already?"

"My precious, how can you ask such a thing!"

"I was...so afraid of doing...something...wrong."

"You were perfect in every way! Everything a man could ask for in a woman, and I swear to you that I have never before felt like this in my whole life!"

Lydia pressed her lips against his shoulder. Then she said:

"When you...made love to me...it was the most...wonderful thing I could...ever imagine...I did not know...love was...like that."

"Like what?"

"A tingling excitement...and at the same time...so intense and vivid that the rapture of it was...almost a pain."

"That is what I wanted you to feel," he said. "Our love, Lydia, is not something soft and gentle. It is strong and resilient, the Power which you spoke of, and irresistible."

"I am sure Love is Life," Lydia whispered, "and that is why everybody...seeks it, knowing that it is...part of God and therefore...part of...creation."

He pulled her against him.

"I adore you," he said. "You always say the things I want to hear, the things I am striving to put into words for myself. My adorable wife, it is wonderful being married to you, because we not only have so much loving to do together, but also so much thinking."

Lydia laughed.

"I am sure no newly marrieds have ever said that to each other before!"

"Well, I have said it now," the Earl remarked, "and it is true. I have never before known a woman I could think with!"

"Then please go on thinking with me," Lydia pleaded, "because it is very exciting . . . although not quite as wonderful as your kisses!"

She lifted her mouth to him as she spoke and he looked down at her for a long moment before he said:

"We said last night that we have found the Island of Love. I think, my darling, that wherever we go our Island will go with us because it is in our hearts, in our minds and it is part of us as we are part of it."

"That is what I will pray for . . . for ever and . . . ever!"

She pulled the Earl's head down to hers as she spoke, and as he kissed her she could feel the strange rapturous flames of love moving within her, and knew they were moving in him too.

He kissed her neck and as he felt her whole body quiver he asked:

"Does that excite you, my sweet?"

"It makes me . . . feel . . . very strange."

"How?"

"Like flames . . . running through my . . . breasts."

His lips moved to the little valley between them.

Now the breath was coming fitfully through her lips and she whispered:

"Is it wrong of . . . me to feel so . . . excited and . . . wild?"

"Not wrong, my precious, but right! It is how I want you to feel."

"Oh, my darling husband . . . it is so wonderful . . . but I . . . want to . . . ask you something . . ."

"What is it?"

Lydia's voice was very low as she said:

"Do you think . . . because you have . . . loved me . . . we will have . . . a baby?"

"Is that what you want?"

"It would be so, so . . . marvellous if I could give you . . . a son!"

It was as if what she had said made the flames within the Earl burst into a raging fire.

He was kissing her wildly, passionately, demandingly. She now gave the complete surrender of herself, not only with her body, but with her mind and soul.

The fire grew in intensity as they drew closer and even closer and his heart was beating on hers.

They were being moved by a Power that had watched over them, guided and inspired them, and which now joined them together in an Island of Love which was theirs for all eternity.

ABOUT THE AUTHOR

Barbara Cartland, the world's most famous romantic novelist, who is also an historian, playwright, lecturer, political speaker and television personality, has now written over 370 books and sold over 370 million books the world over.

She has also had many historical works published and has written four autobiographies as well as the biographies of her mother and that of her brother, Ronald Cartland, who was the first Member of Parliament to be killed in the last war. This book has a preface by Sir Winston Churchill and has just been republished with an introduction by Sir Arthur Bryant.

Love at the Helm, a novel written with the help and inspiration of the late Admiral of the Fleet, the Earl Mountbatten of Burma, is being sold for the Mountbatten Memorial Trust.

Miss Cartland in 1978 sang an Album of Love Songs with the Royal Philharmonic Orchestra.

In 1976 by writing twenty-one books, she broke the world record and has continued for the following seven years with twenty-four, twenty, twenty-three, twenty-four, twenty-four, twenty-five, and twenty-three. She is in the *Guinness Book of Records* as the best-selling author in the world.

She is unique in that she was one and two in the Dalton List of Best Sellers, and one week had four books in the top twenty.

In private life Barbara Cartland, who is a Dame of the Order of St. John of Jerusalem, Chairman of the St. John Council in Hertfordshire and Deputy President of the St. John Ambulance Brigade, has also fought for better conditions and salaries for Midwives and Nurses.

Barbara Cartland is deeply interested in Vitamin Therapy and is President of the British National Association for Health. Her book *The Magic of Honey* has sold throughout the world and is translated into many languages. Her designs "Decorating with Love" are being sold all over the U.S.A., and the National Home Fashions League made her in 1981, "Woman of Achievement."

Barbara Cartland's Romances (a book of cartoons) has recently been published in Great Britain and the U.S.A., as well as a cookery book, *The Romance of Food*, and *Getting Older, Growing Younger*.

More romance from

BARBARA CARTLAND

Moonlight on the Sphinx

*Another sensational
new Camfield novel to add to your
Barbara Cartland library*

Octavia Burke is a proud, beautiful outcast
from her native England. Kane Gordon is
the renegade stranger who holds the secret
to an ancient tomb's treasure. Together
they sail from Alexandria to Cairo, and
into a treacherous plot that would threaten
her life and the Crown.

___ 07732-1   MOONLIGHT $2.50
ON THE SPHINX

Prices may be slightly higher in Canada.